**TANDEM**

The Wizard of Lemuria

The tall, robed figure was old—how old,
Thongor did not venture to guess, but the stamp
of centuries was in his lined face. His eyes were
wise and cool, black in colour and magnetic
with energy. On his fingers he wore many
sigils and talismanic rings, one of iron graven
with wedge-shaped runes, another of blood-red
jade, embossed with a Name of Power. With
these rings, Thongor suspected, the old man
could summon and command spirits and elements.

Unobtrusively, Thongor of Valkarth kept
his hand on his longsword. He was no friend to
wizards, and all his clean Northland blood
distrusted the devilish arts of magic and
warlockry. The fame of this particular wizard
had penetrated even to the remote lands of
Thongor's birth. Sharajsha the Great he was
named—among the most powerful of enchanters.
Some called him the Wizard of Lemuria.

Other titles in this series:

THONGOR OF LEMURIA
THONGOR AGAINST THE GODS
THONGOR IN THE CITY OF MAGICIANS
THONGOR AT THE END OF TIME
THONGOR FIGHTS THE PIRATES OF TARAKUS

The Wizard of Lemuria

Lin Carter

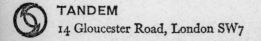

TANDEM
14 Gloucester Road, London SW7

First published in the United States by Ace Books,
Inc., 1965

First published in Great Britain by Universal-Tandem
Publishing Co. Ltd., 1970
Reprinted March 1973

Copyright © 1965 by Ace Books, Inc.

To L. Sprague de Camp
for several good reasons . . .

Made and printed in Great Britain by
Hunt Barnard Printing Ltd., Aylesbury, Bucks.

Introduction

HALF A MILLION years ago, on the Lost Continent of Lemuria in the Pacific, the first human civilisations arose from the red murk of barbarism. For a thousand years the first men had struggled heroically to overcome the Dragon Kings—a cruel reptilian race which had ruled the Earth during the Age of Reptiles—but at last The Thousand Year War was done and the Dragon Kings were destroyed, or driven from the land.

And so began Nemedis, the First Kingdom. Over the centuries her children spread slowly throughout the vast, untamed jungle-lands and across the huge mountains of prehistoric Lemuria; and kingdoms were founded . . . and fought . . . and fell. But with enormous slowness civilisation began to grow, and before long the first great Empire would unite these tiny, warring kingdoms into one mighty power.

It was an age of warriors, when brave men and beautiful women, savages and savants, wizards and champions struggled to carve a red path that led to the Throne of the World. It was an age of legends and heroic sagas, too.

And this is one of them. . . .

"All day our swords drank deep and long
Of blood wine-red, of blood wine-strong!
Tonight in the red halls of hell
We'll feast with foes and friends as well!"

War Song of the Valkarthan Swordsmen

THONGOR OF VALKARTH ducked as the heavy wine-goblet hurled harmlessly over his head, ringing against the wall and splattering cold wine over his face and naked chest. He blinked the cold, stinging fluid from his eyes expressionlessly.

Jeled Malkh, the Otar who had flung the goblet, threw back his head and laughed.

"That is how a noble of Thurdis treats a nameless dog of a mercenary!" he sneered to his companions. They echoed his laughter.

"Pity to waste good *sarn*-wine," one remarked wittily. "Cheap ale of the Northlands is more his drink!"

Jeled Malkh shrugged. "Imagine the lout daring to ask for the payment of his wager—and from the Otar of his own hundred!"

The cold *sarn*-wine dripped down Thongor's mighty chest. He continued to regard the officer. His dark, tanned face was without expression, but those

6

who knew him well could have read the cold glint in the strange golden eyes of the silent barbarian from the Northlands of Lemuria. With one hand he brushed the wine from his face, tossing back his long mane of black hair. He addressed Jeled Malkh quietly.

"You refuse, then, to pay the wager?"

"Yes, I refuse! The zamph with red trappings would have won easily enough, had not that fool Var Tajas ridden him so incompetently. I was cheated!"

Thongor nodded. "Very well then, Otar, I withdraw my claim. Moreover, I will even repay you for the goblet of wine you wasted upon this dog of a mercenary, who is indeed, as your friend said, more used to the thin ale of the Northlands than the scented puke you Thurdans call *sarn*."

While the group of officers gaped with astonishment, the giant Valkarthan moved. With one stride he stepped before the Otar, picked him up, turned him head-down, and pushed his face up to the ears in the great bronze wine-bowl. He held the noble's head under, ignoring his kicks and writhings. When he released him again, Jeled Malkh slumped over the table, white-faced beneath dripping wine, gasping for breath.

In the astounded silence, Thongor laughed.

"Aye, I hold no grudge, Otar. And I have even given you a bigger drink of wine than you gave me!"

Sobbing with rage, Jeled Malkh whipped out his blade and plunged it across the table at Thongor's naked breast.

7

The giant Northlander sprang backward lightly, his own longsword hissing from its scabbard. The officers scattered as the two blades flashed and rang. They circled about the table, feeling out with delicate steel the firmness of each other's guard.

Although a grim smile played about his lips, Thongor was inwardly cursing. Gorm take his hot, Valkarthan temper! He was a thrice-damned fool to pick a duel with his own captain. But—he was in it now, and could not easily get out.

Steel rang against steel as the barbarian mercenary and the jewelled scion of the noblest house in all Thurdis fought. Jeled Malkh was no mean swordsman. His education, as only heir to the House of Malkh, had brought him under the tutelage of the most famed sword-masters in all the realm. But Thongor of Valkarth had virtually been born with a longsword in his hand. In the years of his wanderings and wars as a vagabond, hired assassin, thief, and now mercenary, he had learned every trick of swordplay with every type of weapon. . . .

He toyed with Jeled Malkh for a while, just long enough to please the Otar's self-esteem—then, with a clever twist of the wrist, disarmed him. The rapier rang on the stone flags of the barracks.

The Otar's hand snaked for the hilt, but Thongor's booted foot came down on the blade of the weapon.

"Shall we not end it here, Otar? And cool our tempers while we drink a cup of wine? Come! I acknowledge my hot-headed temper—let us be friends."

Jeled Malkh's thin lips writhed back in a snarl.

"Dog of a Northlander bitch! I'll cut out your putrid heart and feed it to my zamph, for this insult!"

The Otar spat in his face, and thudded one knee into Thongor's groin. The Valkarthan sagged against the table, clutching his gut. In a flash, the Otar snatched up his sword and sprang upon him. The table went over with a crash. The great bronze wine-bowl clanged on the stone floor, splattering them all.

Now Thongor was angry. A familiar red haze thickened before his strange golden eyes, and his teeth were bared in a fighting smile. His great longsword battered the slim Southland blade aside and he set his point against Jeled Malkh's panting breast.

"Enough, I say! An end, or I'll spit you on my steel!"

The heir of Malkh paled. He licked cold lips. The Valkarthan applied a slight pressure. The point broke skin, and drew a scarlet thread down the Otar's breast.

"P-peace, then," Jeled Malkh gasped.

"You swear it?"

"It is sworn!"

Thongor put up his sword and extended his hand for the grip of peace. But the proud noble could never accept defeat from one of his own swordsmen. He seized Thongor's wrist, set his foot behind his heel, and twisted suddenly. The giant barbarian crashed to the floor and Jeled Malkh's slim blade flashed towards his throat.

Thongor smashed the blade aside with one arm, ignoring the needle of cold fire that ripped his flesh.

He sprang cat-like to his feet and, before his opponent could regain his stance, the great Valkarthan long-sword sank to its hilt in his heart.

Jeled Malkh swayed, mouth open, gasping. His eyes goggled, glazing, staring blankly down at the sword hilt protruding from his chest. With one strengthless hand he plucked feebly at the hilt. Then his knees buckled, a gush of blood flooded from his open mouth, and he sprawled on the floor at Thongor's feet—dead.

The mercenary set his heel against the corpse's belly and tugged the sword free, wiping it dry on the dead man's cloak. Holding it, he glanced about the room at the white faces. No one dared to speak. He shrugged, and slid the weapon back in its scabbard.

A sandal rasped against the floor behind him. But before Thongor could turn, a heavy cudgel crashed against his skull. He fell face-forward into a sea of blackness.

Thongor awoke groggily with an ache in his skull. He was shackled to the wet stone wall of a dungeon cell, far below the citadel of Thurdis. Through a trap in the ceiling a lonely beam of sunlight fell slanting, and from its angle he estimated he had been unconscious somewhat less than an hour. It was now an hour before sunset, or thereabouts.

He examined his chains and found them too strong for even his giant strength to break. Then he simply shrugged, with the fatalistic philosophy of the North that wastes no time worrying over what cannot be helped. He was a trifle surprised to find himself still alive. Jeled Malkh's friends and co-officers could well have put an end to him with one stroke of a dirk while he had been unconscious. A slight, grim smile touched his lips. Doubtless the prospect of seeing him chained to the oar-benches of a Thurdan galley for the rest of his life, or watching him fed to the Sark's private garden of vampirous *slith*-flowers appealed more to their cultured cruelty and sadism than dispatching him cleanly with the stroke of a knife.

His scabbard, of course, was empty and he became increasingly aware of another emptiness, that of his belly. About this time of the day he was used to a tankard of sour ale and a roast bouphar-haunch, which he was accustomed to share with Ald Turmis and his other comrades at the Inn of the Drawn Sword. *Well, what you want in this life you must try to get*, he thought to himself.

He bellowed until the jailer came shuffling, fat-bellied and smelling of dream-lotus, to the door of the cell. He peered in at the bronzed giant chained to the wall.

"What do you want?"

"Something to eat," Thongor said. The fat jailer gaped, then snorted with laughter.

"Food, eh? Within the hour you go before the Daotar to be judged for killing your commander—and all you can think of is something to fill your belly! Perhaps you would like a banquet served to you from the Sark's kitchens?"

Thongor grinned. "Why not? I did the city a service in ridding it of a cheat, a coward and a bad captain. Both the Daotar and Phal Thurid, Sark of Thurdis, should reward me for that."

The jailer snorted, "Aye, Northlander, they'll reward you all right—by feeding your heart to the *slith*! Know you not that the Daotar of the Guards, the noble Barand Thon, is the oldest friend of the father of the man you slew? Aye! We'll watch you wriggling while the vampire-flowers devour your flesh—that will be your reward!"

"That may be as it will," Thongor grunted. "But it does not change the fact that I am hungry. Before they feed me to the *slith*, at least let them feed me!"

The jailer grunted with annoyance, but shuffled off, to return a few moments later with a jug of sour, cheap wine and a meat stew. He let himself into the cell and set them down before the Valkarthan.

"Your chains are long enough to reach that," he wheezed. "Yell when you are through—and, by the Gods, be certain you are through before the Daotar's men come to drag you off for trial. I don't want my superiors to think I coddle scum like you!"

The chains were indeed long enough, and Thongor devoured the stew hungrily, and tossed down the cheap wine in two huge gulps. He could always think better with a full belly, and now that his hunger was appeased he began to search his wits for a way out of this predicament. He had been in—and out—of the prisons of a dozen cities in his long career, and he knew as many ways to escape. His first thought was to slump back against the stone wall as if asleep, and

when the jailer came to collect the bowls, to seize him
with his unchained legs and force him to surrender
the keys.

He examined this plan for a time, and then dis-
carded it in favour of another. If his chains were long
enough to allow him to reach the food on the floor,
they were long enough to gather a heavy length into
one hand and smash the jailer over the head with—
at least it was worth a try. Thongor had served on
the galleys of the sadistic Sark of Shembis at one
time, and had no desire to do so again.

He yelled for the jailer, saying his meal was done,
and gathered a long strand of the iron chain into one
hand. The sun was setting now, and the long shaft of
rosy light was almost gone. The cell was gradually
filling up with darkness, and Thongor thought it
likely the fat jailer would not see the handful of
chains. He yelled out again ... and then his alert
senses detected swift, light footsteps approaching
down the corridor. The clank of a key in the lock,
and the door screeched open. The cell was so dark by
now that Thongor could not even see the jailer's face
as the man entered the cell. He watched the dark
figure come near, and his giant muscles tensed, ready
to swing the loop of chain against the guard's skull.

"*Thongor?*"

He grunted in astonishment.

"It is I—Ald Turmis."

"By Gorm! What are you doing here?"

His friend laughed softly. "Did you think I would
let them send my best friend to the galleys? Here—I

took the key, and brought your sword. Quickly!"

Thongor smiled. Ald Turmis, although a thin-blooded Thurdan with Southlander cravings for peace and comfort, was every inch a fighting-man. He was the first friend Thongor had made in all Thurdis, and the best. And now he had come within a hair-breadth of bashing his skull in with a length of chain!

"How'd you get the key?" he asked, as Ald Turmis bent to unlock his chains.

The Thurdan grinned. "The jailer, in his present state, had no use for them, so I brought them along."

"I hope you didn't have to slay him. He fed me well."

His friend laughed. "Just like a barbarian North-lander—always thinking of your gut! No, fear not, the fellow is merely enjoying a little nap. Ah—there!"

The chains rang loosely on the stone floor. Thongor stepped away from the wall, flexing his mighty limbs appreciatively. Untamed barbarian wanderer that he was, he hated being caged and fettered as much as any wild beast.

Ald Turmis handed him the great longsword. "Here's your uncouth Valkarthan blade, and a dark cloak to hide your ugly face in. Now hurry! Barand Thon's men will be here in a moment to drag you off, and we must be gone."

They slipped from the cell, down the dark corridor and through the guardroom, where the fat jailer lay unconscious, and on through a maze of well-lit but empty corridors until Ald Turmis halted before a small, low door.

"You can get out into the side-street this way," he said.

Thongor nodded. "My thanks to you, Ald Turmis. I shall not forget your friendship."

"Nor shall I, and I shall miss you at the Inn of the Drawn Sword, hereafter. But now—hurry. You can steal a zamph from the prison stables and get out of the Caravan Gate before the alarm spreads."

"Aye."

"Where shall you go, Thongor?"

Thongor shrugged. "Wherever they need a strong arm and a good sword. Zangabal, perhaps, or Cadorna. A good swordsman seldom lacks for employment."

"Then farewell. I doubt that we shall meet again, Thongor of Valkarth."

The barbarian wrung his friend's hand silently. He clapped one hand on his brawny shoulder in a gesture of farewell, and passed through the small door, melting into the thick purple shadows of the cobbled street beyond.

Black Wings Over Chush

"The War-Maids rode the iron sky—
Come, brothers, either slay or die!
A dark wing sank as each man fell,
To bear our spirits home to hell!"

War-Song of the Valkarthan Swordsmen

BEYOND THE door, Thongor found himself in a narrow alley between the citadel and a vast warehouse. At the end of the passageway, he could see the stables. Behind the huge pens the great dragon-like shapes of the zamphs stirred. Two bored guards lounged against the rail, watching the huge beasts. Their backs were to Thongor, and with a single stroke he could probably . . .

Then, with a metallic scream the alarm gongs sounded. Thongor repressed a curse. The Daotar's men had reached his cell and found it empty—or had seen the unconscious jailer. The alarm had sounded just a moment too soon, for in a few steps he would have been up to the guards and could have slain them. Now, however, they were alerted, and with drawn blades they stood on either side of the gate to the pens. Other guards hurried from the rear portal of the citadel to reinforce the stable guards. An escaped prisoner would, of course, seek to steal a mount the very first thing.

Thongor ground his teeth with a bitter Valkarthan oath. They could not see him here in the thick darkness of the alley, but how in the name of all the nineteen Gods was he to get away? Desperately he cast his eyes from side to side—and then glanced up. A slim metal shape met his gaze, gleaming in the light of roof-torches.

A malicious gleam danced in Thongor's golden eyes. The very thing! There on the roof of the citadel was moored the first prototype of the Sark's new floater, the marvellous flying boat with which Phal Thurid planned to conquer the whole of Lemuria. The Sark's wise alchemist, Oolim Phon, had devised the weird air boat out of *urlium*, the weightless metal. It was driven by simple rotors, and although the Valkarthan had not the dimmest notion how to pilot the strange craft, he would soon learn. And what a stroke! To escape by the Sark's prized air boat—the only one in existence as yet! It would fly him far above the towers and walls of Thurdis and on to his destination faster than the swiftest zamph in Phal Thurid's pens.

With keen eye he measured the citadel's wall. The fortress was built of great blocks of grey stone, half the height of a man, with an inch or so of space between them. Accustomed from boyhood to climb over the slippery ice-walls of the great glaciers of his polar homeland, hunting the savage snow-apes for their precious furs, it would be far easier for him to

17

scale this wall than for another man.

For Thongor, to conceive of a plan was to attempt it. Swiftly he removed his boots. Knotting the thongs together, he slung them over his shoulder and tossing back the great cloak, he caught the upper ledge of the first stone and drew himself up hand over hand. His bare toes clinging to the small gap between the stones, he ascended, stone by stone.

The air was chill with the night wind from the southern sea, but luckily the great golden moon of Lemuria was hidden behind a thick wall of clouds. There were guards on the roof, and it would never do for them to sight him climbing. With hands and feet fully occupied, he was in a bad position to fight.

Up and up he went, like a great black spider on the grey stone wall. The streets of Thurdis were far beneath him now. One slip, and he would dash out his brains against the slimy cobbles far below. He breathed calmly and deeply, ignoring the pain in his slashed arm.

Then a loose bit of cement slipped beneath his foot, rattling down to the alleyway. For a long second he dangled, feet free, his entire weight supported by his fingertips. Then he clenched his teeth, and drew himself up again, slowly, inch by inch, to a secure foothold.

He clung against the wall for a moment, catching his breath and resting his arms. Above, on the parapet, two roof-guards leaned their elbows against the wall, idly looking out over the city. All they had to do was to glance downwards and they could not fail to see him, a black-cloaked shadow against the grey stone. He held his breath as they talked idly, gazing out over the towers and spires of Thurdis. His arm and shoulder muscles ached from the strain. It was as if red-hot needles were slowly being thrust into his thews.

Still they leaned against their arms, just above him. He could even hear their conversation—as to which prisoner had escaped. The shorter one wagered it was the Northlander mercenary.

"You remember the great lout, the one who made a wager with Jeled Malkh that his racing-zamph would not win in the arena yesterday? He struck the noble Otar down with his great barbarian pig-sticker when the Otar refused to pay! I hear Jeled Malkh nearly stuck the pig himself, but the oaf threw wine in his face, or something. *Hah*! It would be an Otarship for us, Thulan Htor, if we captured the Northland wretch."

"Aye," his companion grunted. "But the street patrols will get him, not you and I. He will steal a zamph and make for the Caravan Gate, doubtless— unless he purchases a hide-away in the Thieves' Quarter. I would like to come face to face with the mercenary pig myself, that I would. I'd show him what Thurdan steel can do with Northlander meat!"

Just as Thongor's arms were about to give way, the two turned away, leaning their backs against the parapet. Silent as a shadow, the Northlander ascended the wall behind them, grinning wolfishly.

The two were still conversing, when a deep voice

spoke softly behind them:

"The Gods have granted your dearest wish, Thulan Htor. Here is your chance to show a mercenary pig what Thurdan steel can do."

They whirled—to see a bronzed giant, naked save for leather clout and black cloak, standing atop the parapet, a longsword in his hand. Golden eyes blazed in a clean-shaven face, and a long, wild mane of black hair fell to the naked shoulders.

Paralysed, they gasped at this phantom that had appeared out of thin air by some supernatural force. Thongor kicked one in the throat, knocked him sprawling. His longsword flashed out to open the other's throat from ear to ear. He sprang over their sprawled forms to the roof.

But there were other guards. A shout rang up— swords flashed in the torch-light. Thongor ran across the roof of the fortress.

The Sark's floater was tethered to a mooring-mast in the centre of the roof, drifting weightlessly some twenty feet from the rooftop. A thick cable was knotted about the middle of the mast, and its other end was fastened to a ring in the rail of the floater's small deck. Thongor sprang up and seized the rope, longsword clenched between his teeth. He slung himself up the rope hand over hand, swinging over the rail on to the deck before anyone could stop him.

One slash of the sword cut the cable, and the air boat drifted free, out over the street. Thongor went across the narrow deck which wobbled beneath his feet, and slid into the small enclosed cabin. His eyes raked the few, simple controls, while the alarm gongs roared behind him and men shouted.

The floater was rendered completely weightless by its *urlium* hull, a gleaming sheath of blue-white metal. The boat was about twenty feet long, from pointed prow to pointed stern. It was driven by spring-powered rotors. One set at the rear, propelled it forward; a second set just beneath the prow, pushed backward; other rotors in the centre of the deck and beneath the keel forced the floater either up or down, as desired.

These engines were set into action by four levers, labelled with the directions which they governed. The levers now rested at the bottom of their curved slots. The higher the levers were pushed, the stronger the rotors drove the craft.

Before the floater had drifted more than a dozen yards from the citadel, Thonger had mastered the simple controls and had the rear motors humming. The air boat flashed over the city, high above the towers. As he passed the mighty walls of Thurdis, Thongor elevated the floater so that they should be well beyond the reach of any arrow. The air boat purred on into the night.

A small oil lamp, sealed in a glass ball, provided light for the tiny cabin. Locking the controls, Thongor swiftly examined the contents of the ship's chest. He found a day's supply of dried fish, a flask of water, and some medicinal salve, which he smeared over his slashed arm. Jeled Malkh's blade had merely laid the skin open.

Clamped to the wall above the floater's single bunk was a powerful war bow, such as those used by the Beast-Men and the Blue Nomads of the far western plains of Lemuria. Phal Thurid planned to mount a fleet of such air boats, manned by crews of archers trained with such weapons, famed throughout Lemuria for the incredible distance over which they could cast an arrow. Despite his fatigue, Thongor examined the weapon curiously. It was the first time he had seen one this close, for his wanderings had never carried him into the western plains where the monstrous and savage Blue Nomads reigned unchallenged among the crumbling ruins of Lemuria's most ancient kingdom, Nemedis, dead now for thousands of years.

The weapon was fully six feet in length, a bow fashioned of the gigantic, curved horns of some unknown beast of the great plains. The extreme toughness of the horn made it difficult to draw such a bow, however, it also gave greater force to the arrow's flight. From veterans of the western cities, Thongor had often heard tales of the fabled prowess of the blue-skinned giants who could reputedly hurl an arrow five hundred yards with fantastic accuracy.

The string of the bow was of fine steel wire, and the arrows themselves were at least half as large as a good-sized spear, tipped with wickedly-barbed points of hard bone that had been honed to razor-sharpness. Thongor looked forward to trying out the weapon.

The floater hummed through the night skies of Lemuria. Now the golden moon broke free of her net of clouds, and lit the landscape below him. Checking the controls to make doubly certain they were locked in place, Thongor went out on the deck and gazed over the low rail at the ground that rushed by beneath him. Far below him the farms surrounding the walled city of Thurdis rushed past—crossed, occasionally, by great roads paved with stone. He could see the farmhouses and outbuildings, plain in the bright moonshine. From this height, they were no larger than the slow wains in which the farmers carried their foods to the bazaars of the city.

It was a fantastic, thrilling experience, to fly like a great bird far above the Earth. Only a couple of men, including Oolim Phon the Alchemist and the Sark himself, had ever flown before. Thongor felt like the hero, Phondath the First-Born, flying through the night astride his winged dragon in the myths. He grinned, feeling the cold wind lift his black mane. Thus the War-Maids rode, bearing the spirits of valiant warriors to Father Gorm, where they should dwell in the Hall of Heroes until vast Lemuria sank beneath the blue waters of the mighty seas!

He gazed above, reading the starry hieroglyphs of the constellations. His father, years past and gone, had taught the boy Thongor to read his direction in the stars—taught him how the two stars in the constellation of the Chariot pointed ever to the Boreal Star. According to star-lore, then, the floater was headed almost exactly northwest. Were he to continue on this course, he considered, he would pass directly over Patanga, and Kathool farther on.

Patanga he had no desire to visit; the city was virtually dominated by the yellow-robed Druids who worshipped Yamath, God of Fire, by burning women alive on his red-hot alters of fiery bronze. Barracks-rumour had it that the young Queen Sumia of Patanga was virtually a prisoner in her great palace, under the command of the Yellow Druid, Vaspas Ptol, who had seized power in the land upon the death of Sumia's father, the late Sark. Phal Thurid, Sark of Thurdis, hoped to wed this young Queen, thus gaining the fabulous wealth of Patanga without battle—if he could wrest the Princess of Patanga from her captors.

Thongor shook his head. The City of Fire sounded too chancy—best that he continue on to the farther city of Kathool, whose Sark needed warriors to protect his jungled borders from the savages of Chush.

He re-entered the cabin to examine the dial that reported the remaining amount of rotor-power in the great coiled springs that ran beneath the deck. A rough estimate gave him five or six hours of flight, before he must crank up the springs again. It would be dawn then. He stretched out on the small bunk and was asleep in a moment.

Below the floater's gleaming keel, the farmlands of Thurdis gave out into wilderness, and soon it was passing over the waters of the Ysaar, silvered by the round lamp of the moon. While Thongor slept the deep and refreshing slumber of one whose strength has been exhausted, the air boat began to cross far above the dense jungles of Chush, and soon the eter-

nal fires on the doomed roofs of the temples of
Patanga passed beneath. As Thongor slept, the
floater hummed beyond the City of Fire, where, unknown to him, his destiny lay, and headed for the
distant realm of Kathool, flying through the night
skies of Lemuria like a great bird.

Attacked by the Lizard-Hawks

"Below him, dark with dragoned fang,
Above, hawk-talons stretched to crush!
Strange battle there, mid earth and air,
Above the deadly deeps of Chush."

Thongor's Saga, Stanza III

THONGOR WAS awakened by two things. First, the
silence and motionlessness of the floater, and second,
the harsh scream that ripped through the stillness of
the dawn. He sprang from the bunk, wide-awake in
an instant. The springs had wound down, and the air
boat drifted without power. But what had made that
raucous screech?

He went out on the deck, and stood amazed at the
unexpected sight. It was the sixth hour, and the
morning sun lit the sky with rose and gold. But beneath him gleamed not the long quays of Kathool,
nor even the wide swath of cultivated lands that
stretched for miles around it. Beneath him lay the
deepest jungles of Chush.

He rubbed one hand against his stubbled jaw, in
puzzlement. He should have left these jungles behind
many hours ago; how could his estimate have gone
wrong? Then he noticed how the floater drifted be-

neath the strong and steady wind that blew out of the east. With a muffled curse to Gorm, it came to him in an instant. When the rotor-power had failed, the weightless air boat had not simply hovered above the regions of Kathool, but had moved slowly west, driven by the strong winds. He was now hours away from where he had wanted to be, above the darkest, most impenetrable jungles of Chush. Nothing to do, however, but crank up the springs again, and head east to Kathool.

But before he could do so, there came again that harsh, metallic cry that had helped to awaken him. Scanning the morning skies, Thongor felt his blood chill as he saw a terrible sight.

Winging down at his floater out of the upper regions was a monstrous and fantastic flying thing. Its scaled and writhing body was fully the length of the floater, and its gigantic leathery wings spread bat-like fully forty feet from tip to tip. Above the body reared a head upon a snaky neck—a head hideous almost beyond belief, with a monstrous hooked beak and cruel scarlet eyes beneath a blue crest of bristling spines. A long snake-like tail floated behind, tipped with a barb the shape of an arrowhead, and cruel-taloned bird-claws reached from beneath the creature's yellow belly.

Thongor had heard of the great lizard-hawks of Chush before but had never seen one till now. They were the fiercest and most deadly fighters of all Lemuria—rivalled only by the mighty dwark, the jungle-dragon itself. And now one was descending with the speed of a lightning-bolt towards his head.

He threw himself flat as the vast shadow of the lizard-hawk's wings fell over the deck. The monster struck the floater a glancing blow and swooped off, climbing for another attack. As the air boat wobbled beneath the first blow, Thongor was nearly thrown off and only saved himself by seizing the rail with one iron hand. He drew himself up as the weird flying reptile came at the floater again. This time it hovered, wings thundering, while it groped for the floater with an outstretched claw. The foot-long talons closed over the needle prow and even the strong *urlium* with which the prow was sheathed was not tough enough to withstand the terrific strength of the hawk's grip. It crumpled like paper.

Thongor sprang to his feet and dived into the cabin, coming out with a length of cord and the great war bow he had found clamped to the cabin wall the night before. While the monster shrieked deafeningly and battered at the sleek hull of the floater, he threaded the cord through his belt and fastened it around the rail so as to hold him securely even if the lizard-hawk succeeded in tipping over the air boat. Then he notched the bow string with a mighty effort, almost cracking his shoulder-muscles, and laid the long shaft of a war arrow across the string.

The first arrow caught the lizard-hawk squarely in the chest. It sank halfway to the feather between the tough snake-scales, and a dribble of green blood ran slimily down the monster's heaving flank.

It shrieked, like a sheet of steel being torn in half by a giant. Releasing the prow, it fluttered away—but not for long. Tracing a wide circle through the sky, the deadly thing came arrowing back towards the floater that drifted helplessly above the jungle.

True to Thongor's expectations, the second blow hurled the air boat spinning end over end through the morning sky. Tightly gripping the war bow, the Valkarthan swung dizzily at the end of his rope. As the floater drifted back into a horizontal position, the flying reptile hovered beside it with booming wings, smashing the sides in with its cruel beak. Dangling at the end of his rope, Thongor sent a shaft winging for the head. It missed the weaving, snake-like neck and hissed on by. But the second shaft caught the lizard-hawk in the throat, just below its powerful jaw. It screeched furiously, mad with the pain of the keen-barbed arrow, threshing wildly with its wings.

One wing caught under the rail of the floater's deck, overturning it. As it spun through the air, Thongor was hurled with stunning impact against the hull. He dangled at the rope's end, unconscious.

The bow and quiver dropped from his hands, falling into the jungle far below.

Hissing with fury, the winged reptile now settled on the upturned keel of the air boat as a bird settles on a branch. Its claws tightened about the long rib of the keel, crunching on the smooth blue-white *urlium*.

Beneath its heavy weight the floater lost much of its buoyancy and sagged down towards the treetops.

Thongor still dangled head-downwards, unconscious.

And now a new danger threatened him. Up from among the trees came the hideous horned snout of the dreaded dwark, the jungle-dragon. It snuffled at the sinking floater. Leaning its forepaws against the trunk of a gigantic lotifer-tree, it extended its sixty feet of mailed neck to the sky.

Lower and lower sank the floater, born down by the massive weight of the lizard-hawk.

As it sank, Thongor's helpless body dangled nearer and nearer to the opening jaws of the dwark. Still stunned from his collision with the floater's hull, he was not even conscious of the approaching head of the monster.

The dwark's entire existence was one unending and continuous quest for food, to fill that huge belly. It was literally capable of eating all day long. More than two tons of meat were needed every twenty-four hours to drive the gigantic muscles in its two-hundred-foot-long body.

The limp form that swung helplessly at the end of the rope smelled like food.

The dwark opened wide its cavernous jaws. Two rows of needle-pointed fangs lined each jaw, and the largest teeth were longer than the Northlander sword that hung at Thongor's thigh.

The yawning jaws came closer, as the dwark strained its neck to the fullest length. Slimy saliva, reeking like an open grave, slid down its scaled jaws. The scarlet eyes flamed with the lust of hunger.

Then another screech rang out. Down from the

sky came a second and a third lizard-hawk. As the dwark paused, scanning the sky above, observing the weird shapes that hovered above, the first winged reptile at last felt the deathly power of the war bow's mighty shaft. It slid drunkenly from its perch atop the crippled air boat and fell flopping down into the jungle, virtually at the dwark's feet.

Released from its burden, the weightless ship bobbed upward again, bearing Thongor out of the jungle-dragon's reach. And into the view of the two lizard-hawks.

While the tiny, dim brain of the giant dwark was striving to understand why its dangling prey was suddenly wafted aloft, far beyond its reach, the scent of the dead lizard-hawk at its feet reached its senses. Abandoning Thongor, the dwark bent to feast ravenously on the dead bird.

Thongor came to his senses, taking in the situation at a glance. Not one, but *two* lizard-hawks to contend with—and the war bow gone, leaving him armed only with his longsword.

And the monster dwark directly below.

He pulled himself up the rope hand by hand and clambered aboard the floater once again, which had returned again to its normal horizontal position. If he could crank up the springs that powered the rotors before the two lizard-hawks attacked, he might yet escape. He opened the trap in the deck, and began turning the wheel. Gradually the long springs wound tight.

Meanwhile the two lizard-hawks circled the float-

31

ing craft warily. Their tiny reptilian intelligence dimly comprehended the fact that this weird invader of their skies had in some unknown manner slaughtered one of their kind.

Red murder blazed in their hideous eyes.

Wings folded, they struck the floater simultaneously.

Still securely fastened to the deck at the end of his rope, Thongor was hurled from his feet by the impact. The ship was batted from the skies as by some monster hand. It crashed prow first into the thick branches of an enormous lotifer—and there it lodged, tightly wedged between bent branches.

The rail crumpled, and the rope snapped. Thongor fell—down through whipping branches, to land groggily on the springy moss that carpeted the jungle.

A hundred yards away, the dwark lifted its dripping head at the sound of the floater's crash.

The lizard-hawks, clamorously screaming in their triumph, circled and flew off.

Thongor unfastened the rope from his harness and examined himself. Despite a number of bruises and small cuts he was unharmed. He crept out of the dwark's view, and was lost in the thick jungle gloom within moments.

Lost, he thought grimly, *is the correct word*. He was marooned in the deepest, most dangerous and impenetrable jungles on all Lemuria—fully one hundred leagues of impassable, dragon-haunted jungle stood between him and the nearest city.

The great war bow that alone might have made it

barely possible for him to stand against the monsters of the jungle was hopelessly lost.

Perhaps even worse, the trees grew so thickly here that he could not see the sky. He therefore had not the vaguest notion in which direction he must travel to reach Kathool or Patanga.

He set out doggedly through the thick underbrush, hacking his way with the longsword. Along towards mid-morning he stopped to breakfast with ripe *sarn* berries and a handful of waterfruit. He jogged along, hoping he was going the correct way, but completely unable to ascertain his direction by observing the position of the sun.

Several times he had attempted to scale one of the giant lotifers that grew so thickly in Chush, their tall boles towering as much as two-hundred yards above the mossy turf. But each tree was thickly grown with the dreaded *slith*, the blood-sucking vampire-blossoms that were the horror of Lemurian jungles. Grimly, he decided not to attempt the trees. He had narrowly escaped death from the *slith* which the Sark of Thurdis kept in his arena ... he would not go out of his way to come in contact with them now.

... *And was it,* he thought, *humanly possible for one man to cross a hundred leagues of jungle on foot?* What would he do during the long watches of the night, still many hours away, when every dreaded predator of the jungles would be out roaming for food? How could he protect himself from the swift-footed poa that could out-race even a trained zamph—or from the man-eating zemedar with its six

33

great arms—or the gigantic flying spiders?

His situation by night would be doubly dangerous, for due to the prevalence of *slith* in the trees, he would not be able to climb them and avoid the beasts.

Still he slogged on. The dense, humid heat of the rank jungle underbrush bathed his naked body in sweat. Time and again he paused to pluck off the huge tree-leeches that clung loathsomely to his arms and legs, sucking his blood painlessly through their microscopic mouths. Once he sank unexpectedly to his waist in a bog, and only saved himself from the sucking embrace of the yellow mud by tying one end of the floater's rope to the hilt of his sword and hurling it into the nearest tree trunk, then drawing himself slowly through the slimy muck hand over hand.

At first he paused to rest only every hour, but gradually, as his iron strength faded under the weight of the oppressive heat, his stops grew longer and the intervals between them, shorter.

As the first touches of darkness fell over the jungles of Chush from the late afternoon sky, he sagged down to the bed of moss beneath a tremendous lotifer, completely exhausted.

He didn't know how far he had come, for he had been forced to detour from a straight path many times, in order to avoid one beast or another, or a group of trees too thickly inter-grown for him to penetrate. At a rough guess, he would estimate that he had covered fifteen miles, perhaps more.

And he did not know if he had been going in the correct direction. If he had been aimed *away* from Kathool, he was a doomed man, for the first city that lay due west was more than a thousand miles away, and his bones would rot beneath the sucking fangs of the *slith* before he could reach its walls.

Then he became aware of a danger far closer.

The distant tread of mighty feet, crushing the underbrush flat, not far behind him. From the way the ground shook under its weight, he knew with a deadly certainty that it could only mean one thing—

The dwark was stalking him.

Dream-Lotus and Wizardry

"... It was an Age of Magic, when the
might of Wizards strove against the
tides of darkness that hovered over
the lands of men like threatening
wings. And the world shall not again
see such wizardry as reigned of old
when proud Lemuria was young, and ere
the Mother of Empires spread her
banners over Aegyptus, young Atlan
and the rose-red cities of the
Maya-Kings. ..."

The Lemurian Chronicles

THE LONGSWORD sang from its scabbard into Thongor's hand. Brush rustled and branches snapped beneath the massive tread. Whether or not this was the same dwark that had devoured the lizard-hawk, the Valkarthan could not know—but it was on his scent.

Danger pumped new strength into his weary limbs. he hurled himself through the jungle away from the monster reptile. Thorn-vines ripped his shoulder with needle barbs as he plunged through them. The thundering tread of the jungle-dragon sounded nearer. It was picking up speed. The earth shook as it crashed through ancient trees, crushing aside patriarchs of the forest that had stood undisturbed for centuries.

As Thongor halted, panting for breath, a soft weight fell over his arm and his senses swam. With horror he saw that he was in the grip of a *slith*. The swaying blossom had opened its soft petals like a yawning mouth, laying bare the triple rows of hollow fangs that could suck the blood from a bull bouphar in an hour.

The vampire-flower emitted a narcotic cloud of perfume that rendered its victim insensible. Senses blurring, Thongor strove to peel the thick soft petals from his flesh. He felt a numbness spread up his arm as the *slith* sucked his hot blood. His knees gave way and he sagged to the springy moss, his arm in the fleshy jaws of the loathsome flower.

As Thongor watched groggily, a faint crimson blush filled the waxed petals. It was his blood, soaking up into the spongy blossom.

At that moment, the dwark came upon him.

Thongor summoned his uttermost reserves of energy. The longsword flashed through the ropy stem of the *slith*, severing the blossoms from its trunk. It continued to cling to his flesh until he tore it off, trampling it underfoot with revulsion.

Still dazed from the vampire-flower's narcotic fumes, Thongor turned to meet the dwark. Seizing the initiative, he sprang forward, swinging the sword. Keen steel bit into the dwark's slavering jaws.

He tugged the blade loose and swung again. The

red sword slashed into the thick folds of flesh at the hinge of the jungle-dragon's jaws. Blood spurted in hot jets, washing Thongor's arm with crimson.

With a thunderous snort, the dwark swung his head from side to side to free it of the stinging pain. The scaled snout struck Thongor with the impact of a battering ram, hurling him a dozen yards. He sprawled on his back, the longsword spinning from his hand.

Before he could rise to regain it, the dwark's dripping jaws opened before him. He could see the curved white sabres of its mighty fangs, as the crimson maw gaped to gulp him down—

"Hold your breath, swordsman."

A tall, robed figure stepped in front of him. In one hand he held a small metal chest. Who—or what—he was, Thongor did not know, but he obeyed.

As the dwark's jaws came down, the old man opened the chest and hurled its contents into them. A thick cloud of blue powder whirled about the jungle-dragon. It swung its head away, as the swirling veil of blue mist entered its nostrils. The fires of ravening hunger died in the scarlet eyes, and, as Thongor staggered to his feet, the enormous length of the dwark came thundering to the ground, shaking the earth as it fell. The beast was either dead or unconscious.

Thongor retrieved his blade and eyed the older man expressionlessly.

"My thanks for your . . . aid," he said.

The stranger combed his long grey beard with slim fingers, smiling faintly.

"The dust of the dream-lotus," he said in a deep, resonant voice. "One grain will transport a man to the dreamworlds of fantastic pleasure within his own mind, for many hours. The dwark has just breathed in enough to render a fair-sized city unconscious. It is unwise and dangerous to wander these jungles armed with the sword alone. But let me introduce myself; I am an enchanter, dwelling nearby. I am Sharajsha of Zaar."

Thongor introduced himself. Unobtrusively he kept the longsword in his hand. He was no friend to wizards, and all of his clean Northlander blood distrusted the devilish arts of magic and warlockery. The fame of this particular wizard had penetrated even his remote land of birth. *Sharajsha the Great*— among the most powerful of enchanters. Some called him "the Wizard of Lemuria."

The Wizard was old—how old, Thongor did not venture to guess, but the stamp of centuries was in his lined face. He wore a long and wide-sleeved robe of neutral grey, and about his middle was a broad girdle of serpent-leather, from which a short sword of peculiar design and a pouch of scarlet *photh* skin hung. His eyes were wise and cool, black in colour and magnetic with energy. An uncut mane of iron-grey hair fell to his thin shoulders and a beard of the same hue fell like a shadowy cataract to his waist. Upon his slim, artistic fingers he wore many sigils and talismanic rings. One was of iron, graven with wedge-shaped runes. Another was of blood-red jade, embossed with a Name of Power. The rest were fashioned of stones, metals and queer woods. With these rings, Thongor suspected, the Wizard could summon and command spirits and elementals.

"You are wounded and fatigued," Sharajsha said. "Let me offer you the hospitality of my home. You need food and drink and rest. Come—my zamph is tethered near."

He would be a fool to refuse the Wizard's offer of a haven, marooned and helpless as he was, many leagues from the nearest city. Shrugging philosophically, Thongor bowed his acceptance. But he determined to keep a wary eye cocked for treachery, and one hand near the hilt of his sword . . . although a Wizard powerful to render a giant dwark helpless would undoubtedly be able to handle a lone swordsman.

Tethered in a clearing only a few steps away was the zamph. This great beast resembled a rhinoceros in form. Its skin was thick and leathery, dull blue in colour and fading to a muddy yellow hue over the belly. Its short and stumpy legs were hoofed with great pads of horn, which could carry it without tiring for days. The snout of the zamph was beaked and from between its little pig-eyes a thick, straight horn grew to a needle-point. Like the prehistoric triceratop which was its ancestor, its neck was covered by a great curved shield of bony substance, like a natural saddle. The rider sat in this bony saddle, guiding the beast with reins attached to iron rings that pierced the zamph's small and tender ears—the only portion of its anatomy sensitive to pain.

Sharajsha's zamph was a gigantic specimen, and its bony saddle was broad enough to seat two. They mounted and set off through the jungle.

"The jungles of Chush seem inhospitable to man," Thongor remarked. "I am surprised that even a mighty Wizard should make his home here."

"Wizards prefer to dwell in remote places of the Earth, so that they can pursue their studies and experiments unmolested and undisturbed," Sharajsha replied. "As I am served and supplied by invisible hands, I require little of cities. Many years ago I constructed a subterranean palace in the hills nearby, and there I have lived ever since. But rarely do I leave my underground abode and venture out into the jungle."

"Lucky for me, that you did so at this time."

"It was not luck, Thongor of Valkarth. I have a magic glass that gives me vision of all that occurs within the shores of Lemuria. By the power of that mirror, I observed your strange flying ship floating over Chush—I watched it attacked and destroyed by the *grakk*, the lizard-hawks, and saw you marooned. I hastened forth to be of whatever aid I could and to examine the wreckage of your flying craft. But that we shall leave until after you have had rest and a good meal."

The great zamph flashed through the jungle aisles. Row upon row of lotifer-trees rushed past, their deep red bark like dried blood in the sunlight. Gradually the trees thinned out as they entered the foothills of a great range of mountains whose grey and purple shapes loomed along the misty horizon. *The Mountains of Mommur*, Thongor thought, remembering maps. He grimaced silently. He had indeed been cutting his slow path through the jungles in exactly the opposite direction from Kathool!

They next entered a labyrinthine canyon that cut deep through the low hills in a winding alley lined by steep cliffs. Blank walls of rock rose sheer a thousand feet, unbroken by any visible door or cave.

Sharajsha reined the zamph to a halt before the wall of rock. As Thongor watched curiously, the Wizard leaned forward and pressed a ring into a tiny depression in the wall. Without a sound, a huge slab sank into the earth.

A black cavern yawned open before them. Sharajsha dismounted and gestured to Thongor.

"Enter.".

He tossed the reins over the zamph's neck, and the beast ambled on before them into the darkness. Obviously Sharajsha kept his steed penned in some part of this cavern, and the zamph was trained to find its own way.

With a fatalistic half-grin, Thongor strode into the darkness with the Wizard behind him. Sharajsha lifted one hand and from the depths of his capacious sleeve drew forth a short rod of translucent crystal. he lifted it and a flickering nimbus of pale blue light glowed forth about one end. It gradually strengthened to illuminate the cavern.

Soundlessly, the wall of rock closed behind them.

Magic! Thongor snorted to himself, with the warrior's natural contempt for such sly trickery. It seemed foolhardy to enter the lair of the most powerful Wizard of all Lemuria of his own free will; and yet . . . the old man had done him no harm, had, in fact, rescued him from the jaws of certain death. *What will happen will happen when it will, if it will,* he thought. And determinedly setting his fears aside with the careless philosophy of the Northlander, Thongor looked about him with interest.

Illuminated by the weird blue glow, the cavern spread before him a fantastic and unearthly panorama. Gigantic dripping stalactites hung from the arched roof overhead—spears of living stone as huge as the fangs of Baroumphar, the Father of All Dragons who devoured the moon in the ancient tale. And the cavern's floor rose to meet them in glassy humps formed by centuries and aeons of those slow, calcareous drippings. Here and there amid the fantastic stone forest, pits of fire glowed and occasionally Thongor saw a jet of yellow flame that rose from the volcanic world of fire that burned far below Lemuria, and which (prophets claimed) would someday destroy the continent, sinking it far below the waters of Zharanga Tethrabaal, the Great Ocean.

"Come."

Thongor followed the Wizard, who led him through the stalagmites. Weird light from the fire-pits painted their rounded glassiness with flickering, fantastic colours. Alertly glancing around, and with one hand resting lightly on the pommel of his longsword, Thongor strode after the Wizard.

It was like a maze, in which one who did not know his way would soon become lost and might well wander for many hours. Sharajsha led him through the stone forest and beyond, where a deep channel cut through the cavern floor. Through this channel a sluggish trickle of hot lava flowed like a river of liquid fire. The slow fluid was cherry-red, and tiny yellow flames flickered about its wrinkled, mud-like surface. The heat rose to smothering temperatures and clouds of thick oily smoke made Thongor's eyes smart. A stone arch spanned the glowing stream, and by this natural bridge they crossed the river of fire. Beyond the lava-river, the cavern floor rose in a wall. It had been carved into a shallow flight of steps, leading to a great iron door set into the wall and rust-red in colour. Rude gryphons, cut from the same rock as the floor, flanked the stair. Thongor glimpsed strange yellow gems set like eyes within the rough stone heads. Was it his imagination, or did a weird spark of intelligence flicker within the jewels? With a prickling of his flesh, he sensed that at a word the Wizard by his side could summon life into those monstrous stone bodies, calling them to his aid.

Sharajsha pressed an iron ring against the portal and with a groan of giant hinges, the huge valves of the gate opened slowly.

Within, the solid mountain had been hewn into a long hall. At its further end, a dais of seven steps was set against the wall, and bore a great throne-like chair of dead-black stone. A long wooden table stood in the centre of the hall. Candelabra of pure gold flickered at either end. Benches were drawn before it. The walls were broken with curtained doorways leading off into other chambers of the subterranean palace, and here and there along the wall and between the doorways, cabinets and chests of wood bore strange secrets. A great circular pit of roaring fire stood before the dais.

"Be welcome in my home," the Wizard said.

Hours later, Thongor and his host feasted at the table in the underground hall. Invisible servants had bathed Thongor's tired body in scented warm water; soothing salves had cleansed and healed his cuts and wounds. He had slept away most of the afternoon and early nightfall on a soft bed, waking with a ravenous appetite.

Thongor's suspicions were relaxing. And the Wizard spread a fine table. Roast bouphar swam in rich, steaming gravy, with succulent, although nameless, fish from subterranean streams. Bowls of weird jungle fruit and platters of sweet-meats were there, and he washed all down with fine wines of classic vintage.

As they feasted, they talked. The Wizard listened to his adventures with a wry half-smile. He expressed great curiosity over the mechanism of the air boat, and strongly desired to see it.

"I am not unfamiliar with this Oolim Phon," he

said thoughtfully. "His mastery of the alchemystical art has come to my knowledge. But he errs in lending his wisdom to the service of an ambitious, warlike Sark, such as this Phal Thurid . . . whose reputation I am also aware of, and his plans to conquer the sea-coast cities. Magic is knowledge; knowledge, in the hands of ambition, is power. And such power, placed in strong hands, could bring all Lemuria beneath one bloody throne. But tell me more of your battle with the grakk, the lizard-hawk. To my knowledge, never before has a single man slain the terror of the skies!"

Their meal complete, they sat at ease before the pit of fire. The hard life of a mercenary warrior seldom afforded Thongor such cushioned ease, and with a full belly and a goodly supply of wine he stretched out like a great golden-eyed cat.

They discussed Thongor's plans. "Kathool is as distant from my palace as Ashembar," the Wizard said, showing him a great parchment map. "I shall lend you a zamph, and, if you will, can help you find your way north to that city. There is a certain path that leads through these mountains and thence across Zand to Ashembar on the River Mahba. But if Kathool must be your goal, you have many leagues of dense jungle to cross. Let us discuss it further tomorrow. Be my guest for the night, at least. And if you would like, tomorrow we shall seek out your air boat. Perhaps it can be repaired and your journey thus eased."

That night Thongor slept a deep and dreamless

sleep, unaware that the inevitable march of his destiny had begun . . . unknowingly, his meeting with the Great Wizard of Lemuria had set his foot upon the first step of a long road, that might lead him either to a throne and glory—or to black and terrible death.

"With dawn we rode from Nemedis in all her
  pomp and pride.
The white road thundered beneath our tread
  and the white sea at our side.
The wild waves broke on the naked rocks
  and returned to break once more,
Where the grim black walls of the Dragon-
  Keep
loomed on the grim black shore."

Doimbar's Song of the last Battle

AN HOUR past daybreak they rose and breakfasted.
The Wizard was anxious to examine the wrecked air
boat, so they mounted two zamphs and rode through
the Chusan jungles, locating the floater without
much difficulty. It was still wedged between the bent
branches of a giant lotifer.

Sharajsha rigged strong cables and pulleys and
with much labour they succeeded in dislodging the
air boat and pulling it down to the ground where the
Wizard could look it over.

"The hull of weightless *urlium* makes the craft
buoyant, and the motive power comes from the long,
coiled springs that run from stem to stern beneath the

deck," the Wizard mused. "Although it's battered, the *urlium* hull still has power to resist the pull of the earth, and the rotors are not damaged."

"You mean the floater can fly?" Thongor demanded. The old Wizard nodded.

"The dents in the hull can be hammered out again, and a little carpentry will repair the crushed cabin. Let us bring the floater back to my workshops."

They fastened the air boat's cable to the Wizard's zamph and bore it back to the subterranean palace, drifting in mid-air behind the great beast.

Thongor looked at it as they manoeuvred the slim craft through the cavern and into Sharajsha's laboratory. The proud, immaculate flying boat that had shimmered in all its sleek perfection above the citadel of Thurdis was a battered hulk. The grakks had sadly damaged it during their attack. The prow had been crumpled like a sheet of parchment, crushed in a giant fist. Sharp and iron-hard beaks had driven in the sides and the cabin had been smashed flat when the ship crashed into the tree branches. It looked a hopeless wreck to the giant barbarian, but the Wizard expressed certainty that he could repair the craft.

"By the luck of the nineteen Gods the floater lost none of her *urlium* plates. Those I could not easily replace. Everything else can be made like new again... and I am eager to examine the structure of the rotors and the control system. Yes, swordsman, in a few days you will be able to fly on to Kathool—or

49

to anywhere else you might desire—as if the lizard-hawks had never driven you from the sky."

Sharajsha put on a leather working-smock and began laying out his tools. Thongor gazed restlessly about the laboratory. Anthanors and crucibles were ranged about on long benches, and tables were littered with odd-looking flasks and tubes of glass. Aludels, curcurbits, alembics and cupels, and other mysterious vessels and devices lined the walls of the long room.

"Can I help?"

"No. Amuse yourself by exploring my home."

His offer of aid rejected, Thongor left the Wizard to his task and wandered restlessly through the strange chambers, exploring the underground castle.

One great room was lined with books of magical science. Books small and huge—some of them as tall as a full grown man. Some were bound in bouphar-leather; others were between plates of worked metal or unfamiliar carven wood. They were written in a dozen tongues, and Thongor, idly opening one bound in the thick fur of a green wolf, was repelled by the weird hieroglyphics painted upon the vellum sheets in inks of scarlet, black and gold.

Another chamber was the Wizard's chemical laboratory. Tanks of green-glowing phosphor fluids bubbled beneath magic fires. Earthen crocks and metal tubes bore seething liquids through the torturous spirals and windings of some strange experiment beyond Thongor's untutored comprehension. A wired human skeleton stood on a rack in one corner. A man's brain hung suspended in a large globe filled with cloudy fluid. Bundles of dried herbs and cannisters of coloured powder filled the air with pungent, repellent fumes.

Thongor wrinkled his nose in disgust.

"Magic!" he growled.

Another room was more to his liking. The walls bore weapons from a hundred cities, clamped with iron to the stone. Swords, spears, bows and javelins ... the crooked dirks of the assassins of Dalakh and the leaf-bladed knives of Darundabar hung beside the feather-crested spears of Vozashpa and the giant war-axes of lost, immemorial Yb. He spent a pleasant hour testing the weight and balance of the Wizard's armoury.

These were all magical weapons, he supposed. Blades were scratched with Northlander runes and the strange, acid-etched sigils of the Blue Nomads of the East. In one sword's hilt a giant ruby was set, gleaming like a watchful eye. It turned in its socket as if to observe him as he passed.

That evening after dinner, as they sat over chilled *sarn* and bowls of waterfruit, the Wizard reported upon his slow progress.

"I have softened the *urlium* prow by heating it in my furnaces, and have bent it back into shape. Now I must do the same for the keel and hull plates. But let us discuss other matters. Tell me, Thongor of Valkarth, what are your plans? Where will you go, once the floater is repaired?"

Thongor shrugged. "Kathool, possibly. Or perhaps

back into the North. A good blade never goes far without finding hire."

The Wizard observed him shrewdly.

"You are then, indefinite? You have not committed yourself to the Sark of Kathool, or of any other city?"

"No. I go where Father Gorm guides me."

"Very well, then. Let me tell you a story . . . and perhaps I shall make you an offer of employment."

Thongor tossed off his wine, and glanced at the Wizard curiously.

"Tell me the story, then."

The Wizard combed his long beard with his fingers, staring thoughtfully into the fire.

"I shall first ask you a question. What do you know of the wars between men and the Dragon Kings?"

"The Thousand Year War? What everybody knows, I know. How the Dragons ruled all of Lemuria before the First Men . . . how Father Gorm shaped earth into human flesh, bled life into it from his own right wrist, and Phondath the First-born lived. How the First Men strove for a thousand years to break the Dragon's hold over the land, and won at last, on the black beaches of Grimstrand Firth, far to the north. Thungarth's son fell there, but slew the King Dragon with his last breath."

"Yes, true enough. You perhaps know that before men came forth from the earth, it was ruled by giant reptiles. Once all of this planet groaned beneath their mighty tread, but today only their descendants—the zamph, the grakk, the dwark and other such—live

52

on. The Dragon Kings were not fairy-tale ogres, but
a race of serpent-men evolved from the mighty reptiles. They were smaller in stature, man-like in form,
and possessed a cruel and cold intelligence, perhaps
as far beyond man's as their life span went beyond
his. When men came forth and founded Nemedis, the
First Kingdom, the Dragons dominated all of the
world, using the strength of their dumb and bestial
brothers to build monolithic cities of black stone,
wherein they practised strange and hideous rites to
dark gods better unnamed."

The Wizard's slow, deep voice droned on, recount-
ing the heroic saga of the Thousand Year War, in
which the sons of Phondath had led the First Men
through centuries of war to win Lemuria for mankind. Slowly the Dragon Kings were beaten back,
although men died by the thousands. But the serpent-
men could command the titanic strength of number-
less reptilian hordes—monsters beside which even the
ferocity of the dwark was dwarfed—and men gradually lost heart. They clung to their walls, in the
ancient cities of Nemedis and Yb, Yaodar and Ith.

"Then their great leader, the Lord Thungarth,
called upon the Father of the Gods. In a storm of
whirling clouds of lightning, Gorm descended on the
heights above ancient and immemorial Nemedis. He
gave unto Thungarth a weapon called the Sword of
Nemedis, the Sword which the Gods had forged, and
in whose steel heart the force of thunder was sealed
by god-magic.

"Armed with this Sword of Power, the last heroes

53

set forth. They broke the Dragon Kings in mighty battles and drove them back to the northern shores of Lemuria, to the Black Keep, the last fortress of the Dragon Kings. There Thungarth fell and the Sword slaughtered the last of the Dragons. . . ."

"I remember the story," Thongor said. And he chanted the lines of Diombar, the Singer of Nemedis:

> *"And Khorbane fell and proud Konnar*
> *and gallant Yggrim too,*
> *Yet still we strove with the Dragon Kings*
> *as the great war-trumpets blew;*
> *And for every hero of Phondath's breed*
> *who on that black shore fell,*
> *We sent a dozen Dragons down the*
> *iron road to hell!"*

The crashing strains of the old war-saga rang out in the flickering firelight, raising dim echoes from the shadowed rafters. Sharajsha raised one gaunt hand.

"Yes, with the strength of the Lords of Nemedis and the magical power of the Sword, the Dragon Kings were slain and their last fortress overthrown, and the five thousand year history of the first kingdoms of Lemuria began. But Diombar the Singer did not know the full story."

"What is the full story, then?"

The Wizard's eyes burned strangely in the firelight.

"The Dragon Kings fell at Grimhaven Firth, yes, but the Dragon Wizards escaped. Transported by their magic arts through the air, they took to hiding far from Nemedis. In hidden castles they survived

54

undiscovered, while the long ages passed by them . . . plotting vengeance with their cold and evil serpent-brains. Ages passed and Nemedis fell, but the Children of Nemedis spread over Lemuria and built new cities, conquering new kingdoms: Valkarth in the North, and Thurdis in the South; Patanga and Cotaspar. And still the Dragons hid, waiting for the moment of their revenge. That moment is very near. Like black phantoms from an age of myth, they live on yet, preserved by their curious sciences. And the hour of doom is coming down over Lemuria, doom not only for the lands of men, but for the very planet upon which we dwell, and the Universe itself!"

Thongor stared at the Wizard. His words seemed fantastic, incredible . . . but they stirred the very roots of Thongor's ancient heritage. For the old blood of the Lords of Nemedis flowed in his Northlander veins.

"Say on, Wizard!"

"The Dragons plot a terrible vengeance that shall not only destroy mankind but wreck the very fabric of the Cosmos. They have striven for long ages to establish contact with their gods, the Lords of Darkness who opposed the gods we worship, the Lords of Light. The Dark Lords ruled Chaos before the Universe was created. When the moment of creation came, they were expelled beyond the new-born Universe, to the thundering Chaos beyond. And ceaselessly from that moment to this, the Lords of Chaos have striven to re-enter space and time, to begin anew their stupendous conflict with the Gods of Men."

"How can they re-enter the Universe?" Thongor asked. Hot blood pounded in his veins. Here was meat and drink for a fighting man's spirit! When gods locked in immortal battle beyond the stars, and all earth shuddered at the far echoes of that conflict . . .

"By some art, the Dragons plot to open a Portal to Beyond. Through that portal the Lords of Chaos may enter space. But the Portal to Outside can only be opened in a certain time, when the cycles of the stars fall into a certain pattern. That dreaded time is drawing near. By my calculations it is very soon to come. It is now seven thousand and seven years since the day that Phondath the Firstborn was given life. In just weeks we shall be into the Hour of Doom. The old year will pass . . . the Festival of Year's End will come and go. It is within the first week of the seven thousand and eighth year of man that the stars will be right for the Dragon Kings to reap their awful revenge upon the world that drove them into exile."

"You know this for a certainty?"

Sharajsha nodded, wearily.

"*The Scarlet Edda* warns of the day to come. And by my magic mirror I have sought out and found the hidden land where the last of the Dragon Kings yet dwell."

He rose and went to a far wall. Opening a chest, he drew forth an old chart, drawn with scarlet inks

56

upon fine papyrus. With one long-nailed finger he traced a path.

"Here is my subterranean palace below the Mountains of Mommur. And here, north and east, the great range crosses Lemuria to its heart. There the vast Inner Sea of Neol-Shendis lies, surrounded by walls of impenetrable mountains. Within the centre of this great inland sea are the isles where the grim black citadels of the Dragon Kings yet stand. And within those towers they work at their hellish craft, preparing to open the Portal to Chaos. Only one thing can destroy them and their monstrous plans."

"What is that?"

"The same Sword that destroyed their power six thousand years ago. The Sword of Nemedis."

"But the Song tells that the Sword was broken in the Last Battle. And even if its fragments were preserved, the Kingdom of Nemedis fell a thousand years ago, and its cities are now heaps of rotting stone."

"True. But the ancient masters of wisdom who wrote the *Scarlet Edda* tell how the Sword was created. It will take a long journey, and will involve many dangers. But I know how to create the Sword anew."

"Is that what you meant when you said you might offer me employment?"

"Yes. I can create the Sword, but not alone. I need the strong aid and courage of a man of many battles to stand by my side against the Dragon Kings."

Thongor bared his white teeth in a fighting grin. Here was an adventure to make all others pale! Here was the raw stuff from which songs and sagas might be made, that man should sing for a thousand years. To hellfire with the Sark of Kathool! Who wants to be a mercenary, when one might become a hero?

"If your words are indeed true, Wizard, and your intentions are as you say, then seek no further. My steel is at your service."

The Wizard smiled.

"I had hoped you would aid me in this task. When I watched you battling the lizard-hawks and the mighty dwark of the jungles, I wondered if you might not be the warrior for whom I sought. Very well, Thongor of Valkarth. It shall be so. But many dangers lie ahead of us!"

Thongor laughed.

"Danger and I are comrades from of old, and many is the night we have stood together, measuring swords. Come, Wizard! Finish your work—repair the floater. Phal Thurid built it so that he might conquer all Lemuria—but we shall see that it serves a nobler cause!"

"The sliding hiss of scales on stone,
    Weird green-flame eyes in shadows black,
When Thongor faced the slorgs alone
    And cold steel drove the nightmares back!"

Thongor's Saga, Stanza IV

THE FLOATER drove through the cool air of morning, three thousand feet above the jungles of savage Chush. Sleek and perfect as on the day it had first emerged from the laboratories of Oolim Phon, it sped across Lemuria. In its cabin, Thongor of Valkarth and the Wizard of Lemuria sat. Thongor was at the controls of the air boat, while the aged sorcerer examined the map.

It had taken the Wizard a full week to complete his repairs on the air boat, newly named the *Nemedis*. Seven precious days out of the small store of time were now spent, and all too soon the ancient stars would return to their foretold positions above Lemuria. While Sharajsha had laboured night and day, Thongor had restlessly prowled the rooms and halls of the subterranean palace, impatient to be away. The giant barbarian was unused to inactivity and chafed at delay. The repairs had taken somewhat

59

longer than had been anticipated, as the Wizard
insisted on installing some devices of his own design,
slight improvements on the original floater. One of
these was a sphere of glass securely clamped to the
control panel before Thongor. Within it a wedge-
shaped pendulum of silvery metal hovered at the end
of a silken thread. This magnetic pendulum,
fashioned of the finest lodestone, was drawn by some
weird influence to the north, regardless of the position of the *Nemedis*. With its aid, one could never
lose direction. The second improvement, of equal if
not superior importance, was a development of the
long, coiled springs which drove the air-screws of the
rotors. In the original model, when these springs had
uncoiled, the floater was without motive power until
they could be slowly re-wound by hand. Sharajsha
had re-installed them in such a manner that the
action of one spring-coil unwinding automatically
wound the second, and vice versa. This gave the
floater ceaseless power, so that the engines would
never die out during a crucial moment.

Sharajsha, completing his studies over the parchment scroll, handed the map to the Valkarthan.

"Here is our present position, marked with a red
spot, and I have noted the pendulum-bearings for the
remainder of our journey. As you see, we must fly
south and east for a thousand *vorn*,* down the Ysar
which splits Chush in two, and beyond Patanga, the

* The *vorn* is a measurement of distance, five thousand five
hundred and fifty-five "strides", or roughly the same distance
as our mile.

60

City of Fire, on to the south coasts of Ptartha, where Tsargol fronts the Sea."

"Aye," Thongor grunted. "But you have not yet explained why Tsargol is our first goal."

"Thousands of years ago a strange object fell out of the sky over Tsargol, which then was but a primitive cluster of miserable hovels inhabited by fishermen. This object was at first considered a fragment fallen from the moon, but the Red Druids, priests of Slidith, the Lord of Blood, called it 'The Star Stone' and claimed it was the burnt-out heart of a fallen star, a talisman of great potency still venerated as sacred to the Blood-God."

"From this stone, then, the Sword was made?"

Sharajsha nodded.

"So states the *Scarlet Edda*, which records the manner in which Gorm the Father of Stars created the enchanted weapon. We shall follow this formula. First we must penetrate Tsargol and cut from their holy relic a fragment to be forged into a sword blade."

"If the Tsargolians worship this burnt-out star," Thongor grunted, "they will doubtless have it well guarded."

"Aye! It is preserved from desecration in the Scarlet Tower, which rises in the temple precincts near the centre of the city and not far from the palace of Drugunda Thal, Sark of Tsargol."

"Guarded?"

"That is the curious thing. No guards are stationed about the Scarlet Tower, nor are any guards—or even the Red Druids—allowed to enter the Tower. It is, in so far as my wizard-glass could see, completely deserted."

"It sounds as though removing a portion of the Star Stone should be simplicity itself, then," Thongor remarked.

"Perhaps. Entering it will be no problem. We shall wait until nightfall and fly over the towers of Tsargol. I shall let you down by a cable into the Tower."

For many hours the *Nemedis* rode the blue skies of Lemuria. The yellow walls of Patanga, City of Fire, fell past beneath them, where it stood at the mouths of the Ysar and the Saan, the Twin Rivers. The floater drove for a time above the great Gulf of Patanga and then entered Ptartha, a vast land of forests and fields with few cities to mar its seemingly endless expanse of greenery.

By late afternoon, they were within sight of the red walls of Tsargol, where it stood beside the thundering shores of Yashengzeb Chun, the Southern Sea. They ate the evening meal and Thongor slept awhile, waiting for the sun to set. As soon as night came down over Lemuria, the *Nemedis* drifted silently down over Tsargol. Fortunately, it was a cloudy night, with neither moon nor stars to betray them to a watchful eye.

Sharajsha guided the craft over the domed palace of the Sark and halted it above the Temple Quarter, where the Scarlet Tower rose from dark gardens. The *Nemedis* was moored to the crimson spire with the sky anchor, a barbed hook at the end of a long line, and by that line Thongor was to descend.

"Remember now, although my glass revealed no Tower guard, it is hardly creditable that the Red Druids would leave their sacred treasure totally without protection. Therefore, be wary! Much depends upon this venture. . . ."

"That may be as it will," Thongor said grimly, as he wrapped his tall form in a black-hooded cloak. "Perhaps the Druids presume it to be too difficult for any trespasser to penetrate the walled gardens of the Quarter, or rely upon religious superstition to protect the relic. However, I have not managed to live as long as this by cultivating carelessness. . If there are guards my steel will feast on their guts."

He swung himself up over the floater's deck. Two hundred feet below his heels the dark garden stretched, a blur of gloom. The cool night-wind from the sea sang about the taut anchor cable.

Hand by hand, he lowered himself down. One slip and he was as dead as Phondath the Firstborn. The slippery cable was difficult to get a solid grip on, but he moved down foot by foot. The strain on his shoulders was terrific, but he kept a clear head, and before long his heels scraped the tiled roof of the Scarlet Tower. This roof was peaked and its conical form forbid foothold. Holding the cable with one hand and the roof-edge with the other, he felt with his feet for the window in which the anchor was hooked for a long, timeless moment—

And found it. He muscled down and slid into a black room. Balanced lightly on the balls of his feet, the longsword sliding into his hand, he waited for a sound, a stir of movement. Nothing came and he breathed easier. He then gave the cable a single tug, by which Sharajsha was to understand that he had entered the Tower without trouble. Now for the Star Stone!

This top room, he soon ascertained, was completely bare. He felt his way into the hall, equally dark, and down a flight of coiling steps to the next storey. There, the rooms contained only books. Feeling his way from room to room in pitch darkness, he wished impatiently for the Wizard's crystal Rod of Light. They had decided that a light was too dangerous, as a passing Druid might see it through one of the Tower's many windows.

Thongor was moving down a hall when the sound first came to his notice. A slow, dragging rasp, dry and stealthy. He stopped cold, listening. The sound was repeated again. It was some distance from him, the full length of the hall. A soft rustle, a leathery slither.

Perplexed, Thongor wrinkled his brow. It was not a footstep . . . it sounded more like someone dragging himself along the floor . . . yet it was not that, for he heard neither the soft thud of palms against the stone, nor the heavy breathing such exertion would have demanded.

Green flames burned, phosphorescent spots of fire against the darkness.

Eyes.

They hung at knee-level, questing the dark. Thongor felt his hackles rise on his neck. His primitive senses gave him uncanny warning—

Again the rasping slither, and the lambent eyes of weird green flame glided forward a few feet.

Serpents? Were the silent halls of the Tower guarded by clammy reptiles? That explained why the Wizard's glass had not revealed tenants in the Tower: needing no light, and dwelling in the dark, they would be invisible.

Silently, Thongor retreated back down the corridor, avoiding a patch of dim light where a window cast vague illuminations on the floor. He waited as the dry rasp continued. And then—

His barbarian blood literally froze in his veins, as the unknown guardian of the hall slid into the light and was revealed in all her repellent, loathly form.

Imagine to yourself a pallid snake as long as a man, upon whose questing and fluid neck grew, not the blunt head of a serpent, but the dead-white head of a woman. Green eyes flamed in a mask-like face whose perfect feminine features clashed hideously with her snake-form. Bald, her round skull gleamed naked in the dull light; scarlet lips smiled, revealing uncouth tusks.

It was a *slorg*, the dreaded woman-headed serpent of Lemuria's deserts. Thongor had never seen one of the nauseating things, but he knew it from shuddery accounts of desert warriors who had felt their clammy embrace in the night.

And now others were coming—he saw their phosphor eyes down the black hall. And he heard the

65

sibilant hiss of the slorg's death-song. They scented his warm blood with their reptilian senses. As the first slorg moved on towards him, he stepped forward and swung his blade. The grey steel whipped through the slorg's alabaster neck, and the terrible head thudded to the floor, tusks clashing, while the severed body writhed slowly in death-agonies.

The other slorgs wriggled towards him, a phalanx of green-glittering eyes and undulant, pale bodies. Thongor turned and raced up the flight of stairs to another floor. He prowled hurriedly through several rooms without finding the Stone. And then the slorgs poured in the doorway in a pallid tide. His long blade reaped a bloody harvest among them.

But now he steeled himself for a feat of utter courage, such as few men are asked to attempt. He had now examined all the upper floors. It remained for him to go down through the lower levels, which meant he must make his way down the stairs covered with wriggling white serpents.

Luckily he wore high boots. He went down the steps at reckless speed, slashing the slorgs from his path as they snapped and hissed at his booted legs. Perhaps the most awful thing about them was that it took them so long to die. Long after his sword had cut through their cold flesh, the heads were sinking their tusks in his boot-heels.

He reached the lower floors drenched with cold sweat, and searched through many chambers, finding only heaps of ecclesiastical robes, or sacrificial weapons, but not the great star-talisman he sought.

And then a flood of slorgs poured hissing into the room, a flood of slithering white serpents so deep he knew there was no chance of making a path through them. So he retreated from room to room, his long-sword dripping with slime and gore. And there in the last chamber his back pressed up against a rough and jagged surface. *The Star Stone!* It stood upon a low, unpretentious altar against the wall, a rough, black mass of metal-slag.

Thongor seized up the mass of cold metal under one arm and retreated on before the rushing snaky-tide. Up the stairs and down another long hall he went, fighting both the slorgs who advanced from below and the creatures who came at him from the darkness of each room as he passed them.

He could move much faster than the sluggish, cold-blooded nightmares, and that alone had enabled him to preserve his life till now. Thongor raced up the last flight of stairs before the oncoming tide, reaching at last the room to whose window the anchor of the *Nemedis* was hooked. Hurriedly, he twisted the cable about the Star Stone and knotted it securely—but before he could climb out of the window, slithering coils closed about his legs. Sibilant voices sang death to him.

He turned, kicking loose, and as he did so the anchor was jarred free, and the cable which was his own path to freedom and the clear airy heights above slid from his grasp. The anchor fell across the dark garden and the *Nemedis* drifted away.

Slimy coils enfolded his body. But, although escape

was now impossible, the Valkarthan's fighting heart swelled with vigour. One last, mighty battle before the end! With a ringing verse of the war-song of the Valkarthan swordsmen on his lips, the giant barbarian turned to fight. Steel rang on cloven bone and thick reptilian gore splattered the walls as Thongor fought joyously, recklessly.

Was it hours that passed, or only minutes? Thongor never knew. Even at the last, as he sank half-smothered to the floor, with darkness overwhelming his consciousness, he was still fighting.

And then he knew no more.

In the Arena of Death

"White sands drank deep the reeking gore
As red steel ripped the scaly hide;
A thousand throats in one great roar
Saluted as the monster died."

Thongor's Saga, Stanza V

IT WAS dawn when he awoke. For a moment he did not realise where he was, and stared around him dully. And then the fog cleared from his brain, and he grinned wolfishly. *In another dungeon*, he thought; *I cannot seem to stay away from cells!*

This one was small and wet, and it stank. He lay on his back in a huddle of wet, mouldering straw. His sword was gone, but at least he was unchained. Thongor came to his feet stiffly and examined himself by the dim red light of morning. Bruises . . . cuts . . . but nothing more. He was faintly surprised to still be drawing breath. Perhaps the woman-headed serpents were trained not to slay intruders, once they had been rendered helpless. Or maybe the noise of battle had aroused the Druids, and they had come to investigate just in time to keep the slorgs from feasting. At any rate, he still lived.

There came the clank of spears and the shuffle of

boots, and the barred door of his cell swung open.

"Awake, eh? Then come along," said the Otar of the spearmen. Thongor made no reply. He looked them over. The Otar was a lean, brown young man with a hard-bitten face and hot black eyes under the brim of a copper helmet. There were seven guards in all—tall, capable-looking men with steel-shod spears. Silently, he stepped from the cell. They formed a hollow square, with Thongor at the centre, and marched down the arched hall. Thongor made no resistance—seven men was just the right number. A few less, and he would have fought. But against seven armed men, he had no chance.

They came into a great hall where many nobles in silks and furs lounged, talking softly. All fell silent as the spearmen led their prisoner to a marble platform, where two thrones of gorgeously-carved scarlet stone stood under a canopy of cloth-of-silver. The Otar saluted twice, and fell back with his men, leaving Thongor alone before the twin thrones.

"Bow to the Arch-Druid and the Sark, you worm!" one of the nobles said, a paunchy man with flabby jowls and jewelled, puffy hands—the Chamberlain, from his silver mace-of-office. Thongor made no reply, nor did he acknowledge the other's remark in any way. He folded his naked arms before his chest and stood tall, feet spread.

"Such insolence!" the Chamberlain cried, and, stepping forward, he struck Thongor with the mace. The giant neither winced nor moved, but stood silently, glowering up at the occupants of the two thrones while red blood trickled down his cheek.

"That is enough, Hassib! Such pride is rare in Tsargol. Let us not try to break it," said one of the two enthroned men. He had a thin black beard, curled and perfumed, and a languid, bored face. His lustreless eyes surveyed the Valkarthan from head to foot, slowly.

From his diadem and intricately fashioned robes, this would be the Sark of Tsargol, Drugunda Thal by name. The other, then, in the scarlet robes, was the Red Arch-Druid, chief of the Red Brotherhood. He was a cold, thin man with shaven pate and colourless eyes. About his thin neck, the great disc of his priestly office hung by a golden chain. It was a medallion of priceless *jazite* metal, glowing with opal hues and worked into a tangled wreath of serpents with eyes of uncut rubies.

"Stubbornness, rather than pride, my Lord Sark," the Arch-Druid murmured silkenly. "We have means to tame such stubbornness. . . ."

The Sark smiled lazily. "Yes, my Lord Yelim Pelorvis. But look at those shoulders—that chest! Gods, but I should like to see that strength in the arena! What is your name, fellow?"

"Thongor of Valkarth."

"How did you enter the Scarlet Tower?"

Thongor made no reply.

The Druid leaned forward. "And where is the Star-Stone? What have you done with the sacred Talisman of Slidith?"

Thongor remained silent. But behind his expres-

sionless face, his mind was working rapidly. He realised that what he faced was not just death, but
torture. The Red Druids would try to torture him
into revealing what he had done with their sacred
stone. While he was not afraid of pain, or of death
for that matter, his Northlander blood seethed at the
notion of torture. When he had served Phal Thurid,
Sark of Thurdis, he had seen what fiendish inventions
the twisted mind could conceive to wring information
from the human body. His soul writhed, sick with
disgust at the thought.

"Answer the Lord Arch-Druid, man!" the Sark
said. "Where have you hidden the Talisman of Slidith, the Lord of Blood? Answer, or we shall have
the truth wrung out of you slowly, drop by drop!"

Thongor was not afraid of revealing the truth . . .
If, as he half-expected, he had been betrayed by the
Wizard, who had flown off leaving him to die at the
mercy of the slorgs, telling the truth would neither
help nor harm Sharajsha. But he was determined he
should not be put to the question. According to the
simple, rude faith of his Northland home, Father
Gorm's War-Maids only carried home to the Hall of
Heroes the spirits of those who had fallen cleanly in
battle. . . . Thongor knew only too well what the
red-hot hooks and clever needles of the torturers
would leave of his healthy body, once they had
begun their monstrous play upon him. Far better to
die cleanly by a spear-thrust, or in the arena with
steel in his hands.

Therefore, he sprang, taking the spearmen off

guard. From complete immobility he flashed into action. Whirling on his heel, he leaped at the first spearman, felling him with a straight-armed blow to the jaw and wrenching the long spear from his slack hands. Whirling again, he charged at the dais. A guard interposed, but Thongor ran him through the belly and the man fell, clutching with numb hands at his tumbling guts. In a flash he was up the marble steps where Drugunda Thal was rising to his feet, features working with terror. Thongor swung the steel base of the spear at his head, knocking the Sark sprawling. The diadem fell tinkling down the steps.

"Seize him! Slay him!" the Sark squealed, frothing with panic. Guards came leaping up the steps, swords out. Thongor whirled to the Druid's throne, but Yelim Pelorvis had melted into the shadows.

Laughing, Thongor whirled to face the guards. He had the advantage of superior height, standing as he did on the top platform of the dais, and he brought it into play. One booted foot crashed into the face of the foremost guard, sending him reeling back upon his comrade's blades, his face a bloody ruin. The steel spear-shaft caught another across the nape, snapping his spine with a *krak*! that could be heard even among the cries and shouts of the crowd. Then he whipped the spear around and caught a third across the throat with a slashing stroke. The man's head was nearly severed from his trunk, and he went down in a shower of gore. Above the clash of steel, Thongor roared out the harsh staves of his Valkarthan war-song:

"Hot blood is wine for Father Gorm!
The War-Maids ride the wings of storm!
Our stout blades their red harvests reap
And thirsty steel at last drinks deep!"

He had slain five of the spearmen when the flat of
a blade caught Thongor across the back of the skull,
and he fell, buried beneath a grunting mass of men,
the bloody spear torn from his hands.

When they wrestled him to his feet, arms twisted
up behind his back, he was laughing.

"I'll wager yon flap-jawed milksop of a Sark never
saw a man fight before, from the way he squeals like
a maiden at the sight!" he roared. "Put me in your
arena with a good sword in my hand, you gutless
virgin-hearted snake, and I'll show you fighting that
will curdle the slimy blood of Slidith himself!"

The Sark was nearly raving with blind fury. To be
hurled from his own throne by a naked and unarmed
prisoner—sprawling on his back, feet waving helplessly before his own nobles, ringed about with
guards! Spitting curses, he staggered over to where
the guards held Thongor and struck him in the face
again and again with his hand, the many gaudy rings
which adorned his fingers cutting into Thongor's
face. The barbarian laughed at him.

"Yes! To the arena with this vomit of the North!
We'll see how this hero fares, pitted against our
pets!" the Sark snarled.

From nowhere the Arch-Druid appeared, laying a
slim, claw-like hand on Drugunda Thal's arm.

"No, my Lord Sark! We must put him to the torment—we must find the Stone—"

"Who's Sark of Tsargol, snake-face?" Thongor grinned. "You—or that slime-eating old vulture? I'll wager he tells you when to change your breeks as well!"

The Sark went livid with rage, spitting and snarling. He shook off the restraining hand of the Druid.

"Drugunda Thal rules in Tsargol, filth! And when you face my pets it is before *my* throne that you shall grovel, whimpering with terror!"

Thongor only laughed mockingly.

"Away to the pits with him! At noon he shall die in the arena, I swear it by all the Gods!"

Thongor was still chuckling when they dragged him away. His ruse had worked. He had not seriously hoped to escape from a roomful of armed men, armed only with a spear himself. His only hope to avoid the humiliation of torture was to enrage the Sark enough so that he would override the objections of the Arch-Druid (who obviously stood as co-ruler here, or at least was very near the Sark in authority). With a barbarian's instinctive understanding of men, Thongor estimated that the Sark—weakling that he was—usually was kept under the Arch-Druid's control by the simple method of having his passions pandered to and encouraged, while the cold-blooded priest ran the Sarkdom.

A fighting grin bared Thongor's white teeth. He had certainly brought his scheme to success! Not only had he maddened the Sark enough to get condemned to the arena, but he seemed to have forced an open breach between the Sark and Druid.

He was still chuckling over that when they hurled him into a cell in the pits below the arena. The spearmen had never before heard a condemned man laughing as he was locked into his cell . . . but then, they had never encountered a man like Thongor before either, and, the barbarian vowed, they had never seen the kind of fighting he intended to do when the hour of contest came!

And it came soon enough. Thongor had barely finished a meal of bouphar-beef, bread, cheese and wine which he had bullied out of the dim-witted old pit-keeper, before another troop of guards came marching in to lead him out. This time there were ten of them, and with drawn swords in their hands. Obviously they did not wish to see another example of Thongor in action!

With them was the same lean brown, hard-bitten Otar who had awakened Thongor that morning. But this time he bore no spear, and his red sash of office was gone. He was a prisoner!

"Why are you here?" the Valkarthan asked, as the spearmen led them out. The former Otar glared at him and said hotly: "Because of you, Northlander lout! I was disgraced that my prisoner should break loose before the Sark—hurl the Sark on his royal face, in fact, while I and my men stood by gaping. So I have been stripped of rank and am to face the terrors of the arena beside you!"

"Well . . . I am sorry for that. I only meant to get

my hide out of the torturers' reach and into the arena where I could expect a clean death," Thongor muttered. "I did not mean to bring another man into trouble by my actions."

The Otar shrugged.

"Ah, well. What matter? It would have happened sooner or later. The Sark hates my family, who are a minor branch of the former ruling dynasty. His father, Thald Kurvis, seized power when the last House died out. The Druids supported him because he was inclined to this bloody Slidith-worship, while my house, the Karvus, ignored the cult. The blood-drinkers did not dare to stamp us out because of the high esteem my father had won in the Vozashpan Wars. Instead they stripped us of power and humiliated us, reducing my father from chamberlain to mere archivist, and myself to Otar, the mere captain of a hundred."

Thongor absorbed this silently as they were marched through winding stone corridors.

"What of your father? Can he not help you now?"

The Otar smiled sadly.

"Nay. He died three years ago—poison, some say. I am the chieftain of my house, and if I cannot help myself, there is no one who can. Well, we shall die together, then. It is perhaps better this way, with a good sword in my hand, facing an enemy that I can see, than being struck down in the dark by an assassin's dirk or a poisoned goblet, which would come in a year or two, when the mighty Sark thinks I am too powerful."

Thongor nodded, grimly. This was the kind of spirit his barbaric soul admired most! He liked the young Otar's wolfish grin and tough-hewn spirit.

"If we are to die together, let me know your name," said the Valkarthan. "Mine is Thongor, Son of Thumithar, a mercenary out of Valkarth."

The youth smiled. "Well met, Thongor. I am Karm Karvus, Lord of Karvus . . . or I was. I shall be proud to fight beside such a warrior as yourself. I have never seen such work as you displayed there in the Hall of Two Thrones. Let us face death on the sands and go down in a battle that shall leave the snake-blooded lords of Tsargol shivering in their robes!"

"It is agreed," Thongor smiled.

"Quit whispering you two!" the new Otar snapped. "Here! Take swords—you, barbarian, take this!" And he handed Thongor his own Valkarthan longsword, which the barbarian had not seen since it had served him so well in the Scarlet Tower. He hefted it in his hand, grinning at the guard.

"The Sark says you will fight better with your own blade in your hand," the guard sniggered. "*I* say you could be armed with thunderbolts, for all the good it will do you when the Gate of Death lifts!"

Beside him, Thongor heard Karm Karvus draw in his breath sharply.

"The Gate of Death? The Sark will pit us against—?"

"Yes!" the Otar sneered. "You will face the Terror of the Arena, Karm Karvus!" Then to Thongor, he said: "It is a great honour, Valkarthan, but one perhaps that a barbarian such as yourself could not appreciate. Only the worst criminals face the Terror of the Arena, and then only on days sacred to the Lord of Blood, the God Slidith." And turning back to Karm Karvus again, he grinned nastily. "It was a happy day for me, Karm Karvus, when you allowed your prisoner to insult the great Sark. Now I am Otar in your place, instead of a mere spearman!"

Karm Karvus laughed. "Yes, Tole Phomor, and you may even become a Daotar in time. Not being a noble such as I, but a baseborn cur, you will never arouse the jealousy of the Sark!"

Tole Phomor snarled a curse, and thrust them forth.

"Go out and die!"

They went out the stone portal into the arena and stood blinking in the sun as the steel gate crashed shut behind them. Karm Karvus hefted his good Tsargolian blade, and glanced round. Smooth white sand, bakingly hot under the tropic noonday sun, stretched to either side. The arena was oval, walled with steep stone along whose upper edge down-pointing iron spikes were set. Above the row of spikes, tier upon tier of gaily-dressed Tsargolians sat, applauding their presence with cheers and boos and laughter.

Thongor blinked against the sun's blaze and stared about him. Straight ahead was the royal box, where Drugunda Thal, Sark of Tsargol, and the red Arch-

Druid sat, apparently friends again. Directly beneath the box was a grim iron gate made in the likeness of a horned human skull, whose gaping jaws were set with heavy iron bars.

The Gate of Death.

Thongor spread his legs and stood waiting. He wondered what would emerge from the jaws of death, what possible beast would the Sark pit him against that could be so terrible as to earn the title of "the Terror of the Arena". He had faced all manner of beast in the past few days, from hawk-lizard to the fearful jungle-dragon. What would come out of the Gate of Death?

Above, in the shadow of the canopy-covered royal box, Drugunda Thal leaned forwards expectantly as the two emerged from the pit's gate. Gloatingly, the Sark ran his eyes over the magnificent body of the Valkarthan, eyeing the smooth, tanned flesh that would soon be torn to ribbons, dripping hot blood into the white arena sands.

"I still say this is a mistake, O Sark," the soft voice of the Red Arch-Druid came to him. "The man should be tortured so that we may learn what he has done with the Star Stone."

"It is the arena for such scum, Yelim Pelorvis, as I have commanded. The Stone was not upon him when he was captured, but neither was it hurled from the windows of the Scarlet Tower into the temple grounds, for all that has been searched. No, the barbarian merely hid it in some corner of the Tower, where it shall doubtless soon be found."

"But what if——"

"Silence, I say! I am Sark over this city, not you, Druid!"

Yelim Pelorvis lapsed into silence, but his eyes were burning with a cold, acid fire and he glared venomously at the Sark. Drugunda Thal stood, magnificent in his gorgeous silken robes, the diadem of Tsargol sparkling upon his brows. He raised one thin arm, imperiously.

"Release the Terror!" he cried shrilly.

Thongor tensed as the steel bars of the Gate of Death slowly, creakingly, rose into the wall, revealing a black pit. Then——

With a blood-freezing scream, a crimson thunderbolt launched itself across the arena straight at them. It was all snarling jaws and glittering fangs. Eyes the colour of yellow sulphur blazed with bloodlust. A wicked barbed tail lashed the sands as it charged with incredible speed.

Thongor froze, every sense alert. It was a zemadar, the most dreaded monster of all Lemuria. The ferocious zemadar was the most deadly killer of the jungles, possessed of an insane ferocity that often made it charge in the face of certain death, capable of out-racing even a speed-bred zamph in the fury of its hurtling charge.

But it was more dangerous still because of its triple row of foot-long fangs, each tusk razor-keen and bearing a poisoned saliva that instantly paralysed its foe. Like a crimson juggernaut it hurled across the sands at them.

Thongor flung himself to one side and ploughed into the sand, the zemadar narrowly missing him. But the beast spun instantly, snapping at the air over his head. He drove the longsword into its throat.

But to no avail. The leathery flesh of the crimson monster was too tough for even his blade to pierce. He leaped backwards as the twenty-foot horror sprang at him, batting the air with steel-hooked claws and growling ferociously.

Karm Karvus had also barely jumped clear of the charge. He brought his blade home against the monster's ribs, but the sword glanced off.

The zemadar whirled, its barbed tail lashing. It knocked Karm Karvus' feet out from under him, and he fell sprawling face-downwards in the sand. The zemadar turned to gobble up its prey.

Then Thongor did a thing so foolhardy—or so brave, depending on your outlook—that it brought the entire throng to its feet with a gasp. In the box, the Sark leaned forwards, in the blood-lust.

Thongor sprang upon the beast's back.

Locking his iron-thewed legs about the base of the monster's neck, he clung to the arching neck, ignoring the ridge of spines that run down its back. The zemadar had never felt a live weight on its back before, and it went mad with rage. It bucked and kicked with a snarling frenzy. But Thongor clung grimly to his precarious perch. He began inching upwards.

"What is that mad fool doing?" the Sark gasped, craning forwards to see through the mad blur of the struggling man and monster. The cold, sardonic voice of Yelim Pelorvis rang clearly: "Climbing up to get at the zemadar's eyes, I believe. They are the only vulnerable portion of the beast's entire body, as he doubtless knows."

The Sark laughed harshly.

"He will never do it! Never!"

Yelim Pelorvis smiled a thin-lipped smile.

"We shall see. I have a feeling that you are about to lose your prize zemadar, O mighty Sark. . . ."

Sweat dripped down into Thongor's eyes and the naked sun blinded him. He clambered up the lithely-twisting neck to the head, digging his feet into the ridges of the zemadar's crimson hide and ignoring its struggles to unseat him. He clamped one brown arm about the monster's upper neck and with the free hand, drove the steel blade deep into the zemadar's eye. It screamed like a great sheet of canvas being ripped apart with one pull.

He dug the point deep, probing for the zemadar's tiny brain. On the sands below, Karm Karvus closed in, driving his steel at the monster's belly.

The zemadar, mad with pain, kicked the Otar away again, and fell backwards, grinding Thongor into the sand. The enormous weight of the creature might have crushed him, but the sand was soft and loosely-piled, so that he merely sank into it. The crowd went mad with the heroic battle, screaming their throats raw under the blazing, noontide sun.

The zemadar staggered to its feet and dragged itself over to the wall. Thongor, seeing that he was doing no good there, slid the sword out and reached for the second eye.

"What is my pet doing now?" the Sark quavered.

"Trying to scrape the barbarian off his back by rubbing against the arena wall," the Arch-Druid observed coolly.

Indeed it was. And it had rubbed Thongor's left thigh raw before the cold steel of the Valkarthan longsword sank to its hilt in the monster's other eye.

The crowd held its breath.

Coughing blood, the zemadar staggered blindly away from the wall into the centre of the arena. Thongor sprang from its back, landing lithely on his feet.

Twisting its gory head from side to side slowly, blindly seeking its foe, the zemadar lurched up to the Gate of Death. Thongor felt a chill run down his spine, like fingers of ice. Gorm! The thing took long enough to die. . . .

It coughed a gush of blood and sank to the sands twitching. The long spiked tail thumped the sands once or twice, raising a white cloud. And then it died.

Thongor, with Karm Karvus by his side, raced across the arena to stand beside the beast. Thongor stared up at the astounded Sark.

"That is how a man fights, Sark of Tsargol. Now let us see how a man dies!"

And he flung the sword glittering through the air. The paralysed throng watched as the blade completed its sparkling flight—and quenched its brightness in the breast of Drugunda Thal, the last Sark of the Royal House of Thal.

The Sark came to his feet, seizing the sword-hilt with both hands, staring at it with goggling eyes. His mouth gawked like a beached fish. Blood came out and dribbled down his thin beard. With a heave of unexpected strength he tore the blade out of his breast. Then he tottered and fell face forward from the royal box, hurtling down to thud against the arena sands, almost at Thongor's feet. The Valkarthan bent down, picked up his sword, and wiped it dry against the dead Sark's bloodied robes.

A tall, thin figure in scarlet robes, Yelim Pelorvis stood alone in the royal box. Slowly he stooped, smiling, to pick up the diadem of Tsargol, which had fallen to the floor when Drugunda Thal dropped from the box. He placed the diadem upon his own shaven brows.

Then the crowd exploded. Guards came leaping down the tiers of seats brandishing their weapons. The nobles poured to and fro, screaming hysterically. Red-robed priests chanted solemn psalms. From the pits across the arena, guards pelted forth.

Thongor grinned at Karm Karvus.

"That was just a taste, friend! Now we are pitted against men, not monsters!"

Karm Karvus laughed, and tossed his sword up, catching it by the hilt.

"Now we shall show them fighting, eh, barbar-.ian?"

And then the sun was darkened. A swift shadow

moved over the blood-dabbled sands. A glittered metal ovid cut the air silently, a knotted rope dangling from beneath its curved keel—the *Nemedis*!

Thongor grunted. So the Wizard had not abandoned him, after all! As Karm Karvus stood frozen, staring up at the weird flying craft, Thongor seized the younger man up, tossed him across his broad shoulders and caught the rope as it swept past. The *Nemedis* turned and climbed steeply, bearing the two off the arena sands—above the wildly-milling crowd —over Tsargol—and off, vanishing into the noonday skies.

The Green Ghosts

"From wild red dawn to wild red dawn
    we held our iron line
And fought till the blades broke in our hands
    and the sea ran red as wine.
With arrow, spear and heavy mace we broke
    the Dragon's pride,
Thigh-deep in the roaring sea we fought,
    and crimson ran the tide."

Diombar's Song of the Last Battle

THEY CLUNG to the line as the floater lifted. A few arrows hissed by them as they cleared the last tier of the arena and then they were out over the streets of Tsargol, where news of the Sark's death had spread, and townsmen fought with Druids till the gutters ran red with blood.

"What is this—thing?" Karm Karvus asked.

Thongor lifted his voice above the roaring winds that sang about them. "A flying boat. It is driven by a friend—a powerful magician from Chush. Have no fear."

As the red walls of Tsargol drifted past below them, the two pulled themselves up the swaying line, hand over hand. They clambered over the low rail and Karm Karvus wiped his brow, staring down at the forests and fields that rushed past beneath their keel.

"His magic must be powerful indeed, to fly like a bird without wings!"

The Wizard was in the *Nemedis'* cabin. They went across the quivering deck to join him.

"Thank Pnoth you are safe, Thongor," Sharajsha said as they entered the cabin. "Who is your companion?"

"Karm Karvus, a noble of Tsargol, condemned with me to the arena. I could not leave him behind while I escaped alone." The Wizard nodded, greeting Karm Karvus.

"Let me salve your wounds," he said, locking the controls on a north-westerly course. From beneath the low bunk he drew medicines. As he applied a poultice to Thongor's thigh which had been rubbed raw when the zemadar scraped him against the arena wall, he said: "I did not know what to do when the anchor became dislodged from the Tower's window. Before I could manoeuvre the *Nemedis* back and attempt to pick you up, the gongs were ringing and the temple gardens were filled with guards and priests with flaming torches. Did you think I had deserted you?"

"I did not know what to think," Thongor admitted.

"I saw that you had tied the Star Stone to the line, so I took the floater up beyond sight and waited for a chance to rescue you. Then I saw you and Karm Karvus here fighting in the arena and came down to help you escape. I thank Pnoth, God of Wisdom, that you escaped with your lives!"

"Thank rather Tiandra, Goddess of Luck," Thongor grunted. "Have you anything to eat?"

All that afternoon the air boat flew above Ptartha, while Thongor and Karm Karvus ate and rested. Sharajsha told the Tsargolian of their quest for the Star Stone and of their plan to overcome the Dragon Kings, and the Prince of Karvus decided to join their adventures. Now that he was a homeless wanderer like Thongor, he said, he could do no better than to assist their cause in gratitude for his rescue.

"By evening we shall be over Patanga, the City of Fire," Sharajsha said. "I have cut a large fragment off the Star Stone, and in the Eternal Fires I must forge it into a sword blade."

"Where is this Fire?" asked the Valkarthan.

"In the crypts below the High Alter of Yamath, Lord of Flame. I have a plan by which we can penetrate the city and, with luck, forge the Sword uninterrupted and undiscovered. But we must wait till darkness."

By nightfall they were high over Patanga. The red-roofed city rose on the Patangan Gulf, between the mouths of the Ysar and the Saan Rivers. As darkness gathered over the sky, the floater sank silently to hover like a ghost-hawk over the spiked domes of the Fire Temple.

"One of us must remain in the *Nemedis*," Sharajsha said. "Karm Karvus, that one must be you."

"It is not my way to remain behind in safety when my friends face danger," the Tsargolian protested.

"I must forge the Sword and Thongor shall guard me; there is none to remain behind, holding the floater in readiness for flight, save you."

"Very well then."

Sharajsha gathered a black cloak about himself, drawing the hood over his features.

"When we are on the roof, take the *Nemedis* up a thousand feet and remain there. We shall signal with this mirror when we are ready to go," the Wizard said, showing Karm Karvus a small glittering disc. The Tsargolian nodded that he understood.

"Let us be gone," Thongor said restlessly. "It is risky having the floater hang here like this, where anyone might glance up from the street below and see it."

Karm Karvus touched the controls and the floater descended, brushing her keel along the temple roof. The two cloaked figures of his comrades slid over the rail and melted into the shadows of the dome. Then he touched the controls again and the silvery shape vanished upwards into the cloudy darkness.

"This way. There should be a door here," Sharajsha said, feeling along the curved dome. He found a secret catch and a door fell open, revealing a yawning square of blackness. They entered carefully, feeling their way.

"This stairway spirals down; be careful and watch your footing—we dare not risk a light!"

They went down the well of complete darkness as

silently as possible.

"How do you know of this way?" asked Thongor.

"Of old this temple was the palace of Zaffar, a Wizard of ancient times. I have read in his scrolls of the network of secret panels and hidden stairways that he built into his castle. This stairwell leads us directly into the crypts below the entire Temple, where the Eternal Fire burns."

"What is this Fire?"

"No man knows. The Yellow Druids of Yamath call it 'The Ever Burning Fire'. It is a jet of some unknown vapour that rises from the secret core of Lemuria . . . or perhaps even from the very bowels of the Earth. It has burned for countless ages with a flame that never goes out. The Cult of Yamath regards it as an oracle and reads the portents of the unborn future by its weird light. I feel it is a natural phenomenon of some sort."

They were now within the very walls of the Fire Temple. These walls of massive blocks of stone were hollow, and between them the stair wound down into the secret crypts beneath. After some time they reached the last step, and Sharajsha felt about for the second catch while Thongor drew his great Valkarthan sword out, ready for danger.

A click and the door opened. They stepped out into a corridor of smooth stone, lit by flaring torches of oil-soaked wood, set along the wall in wrought-iron brackets.

"This way!" Sharajsha hissed.

They slunk along the corridor, standing close to

the wall to gain as much protection from the shadows as was possible. They encountered no guards, and came at length to a great brass door. It was carved and worked with the flame-edged symbols of Yamath.

"No guards?" Thongor grunted.

Sharajsha shrugged. The door was unbolted. He pushed it open and they looked into a great cavern with rough-hewn walls. There in the floor of the cavern was a sunken well. From it dancing flame of weird green could be seen emerging. It cast flickering shadows about the gloomy cave.

"You stand here and watch by the door. I shall go below and perform what is necessary."

Thongor nodded and took his place as the Wizard went down a stone flight of steps into the cavern of the Fire. He held the door open a slit so that he could see out and would detect anyone coming. This complete absence of guards both worried and puzzled him. He remembered the way the seemingly-unguarded Scarlet Tower had contained the deathly slorgs. It was logical to assume that the cavern was similarly protected. Then he shrugged. Whatever might come, his stout sword or the Wizard's magic could certainly handle it.

Sharajsha reached the edge of the well. From beneath his cloak he drew out a fragment of the Star Stone and a hammer inscribed with runes and queer letters of magic writings, and a long-handled pair of tongs. He clamped the tongs about the fragment of unknown star-metal and held it within the dancing green cone of the Eternal Fire of Yamath. Whatever caused this mysterious green flame lent it far greater and more intense heat than any ordinary fire, for the fragment of star-metal soon glowed cherry-red, then pale orange-yellow. The stone hissed and crackled in the dancing green Fire.

A sudden noise—Thongor snapped instantly alert. Putting his eye to the crack of the door he could see nothing. But he heard a soft scraping sound approaching down the torch-lit corridor.

With a whispered call, he informed Sharajsha of this. The stone now glowed pale yellow-white.

"Hold them off!" the Wizard called. He withdrew the glowing fragment and held it over the iron edge of the well. He began to beat the glowing metal with his hammer, and as he did so his lips formed soundless words.

A fat, yellow-robed Druid approached down the hall, accompanied by a dozen guards with plumed helmets. Would they enter the brass door, or go by it to some other room? Thongor's question was soon answered—they headed for the door of the cavern. A guard stepped forward ahead of the Yellow Druid to open the door for him. As he did so, stepping into the cavern, Thongor cut him down with a single stroke. The man's body rolled down the flight of stone steps.

The guards yelled and their swords flashed into their hands. Thongor swung the gates wide and stood there in the entrance, smiling faintly, the long sword dripping crimson. Two guards sprang at him.

Steel rang on steel harshly, filling the hall with iron

echoes. They were decent swordsmen, but Thongor had faced far better. He disarmed one with a practised twist of the wrist and gutted him with a back-handed swipe across the middle. The man fell screaming, and his body blocked the other. The second guard stepped back to avoid the falling body, lowering his guard as he did so. Thongor's point darted forward and sank into his breast.

The doorway was only wide enough for two, and now that the first two had fallen, two others came forward. For a time Thongor was hard-pressed. Behind him he heard the measured ringing of the magic hammer, beating the glowing lump of stone into a sword blade. He fought on.

Two grim-faced guardsmen engaged his sword. Steel flashed and rang in the red glare of the torches. One guard fell with a cloven skull. Thongor's dripping blade sank into the second's chest. But the tough yellow leather of the guard's jerkin caught and held the steel and as Thongor laboured to withdraw the blade, two guards seized him. One held his arms and the other drove a dirk at his heart. Thongor kicked the guard in the face and wrenched free. They were all around him now. His fists drove like mallets, crushing flesh and smashing bones. Then they brought him up against the wall, pinning his arms and legs. The fat Druid came snarling towards him, now that the Valkarthan was helpless. When he had been free, the priest had not ventured within reach of his arms.

"Blasphemer! Desecrater!" he hissed, baring his

greasy teeth. "You dare spatter the sacred crypts with human blood!"

Thongor laughed and spat directly in the Druid's face.

The priest went scarlet to the lips, blazing with fury. He seized up a sword and brought it up in a hissing arc towards the Valkarthan's naked chest—

His hand faltered—stopped. The blade rang on the stone floor. The face that had flushed scarlet with fury now paled with sick terror. The Druid's eyeballs crawled to the left, staring at something beyond Thongor.

One by one the guards turned to stare at the thing Thongor could not see, beyond his shoulder. Their faces blanched white with pure fear. Trembling, afraid to turn and run, they backed away down the hall.

Now free, Thongor scooped up his sword and turned to face—*green ghosts*!

There were three of them—transparent as glass, dim as mist, a weird and sickly green. Their groping hands were bird-clawed. Fanged and dripping jaws grinned in dead mockery from skull-heads. In black eye-sockets, sparks of evil green fire flickered.

Thongor felt his hackles rise, his neck-skin prickle. And the superstitious night-fears of the barbarian rose within him. He backed away, watching as the grisly phantoms advanced. One of them, whose terrible skull-head was veiled behind lank hair that grew from a dirty patch of scalp still clinging to the naked bone, advanced with a hound-like lope. The second slid forward with a snaky grace. The third, whose head had been cut off and was carried beneath one bone-thin arm, shambled along as if crippled. From their hideous green bodies, filthy tatters of tomb-shrouds flapped.

The Druid, his fat quivering face the colour of curds, made the sign of Yamath with a puffy hand. Neither it nor the stuttering ritual of exorcism he next tried halted the advance of the green ghosts.

Abandoning dignity, the priest turned and ran with the guards and Thongor faced the phantoms alone.

He kissed the red blade of the longsword and muttered a quick prayer to Father Gorm. Then he sprang forward. The red steel hissed through the ghosts. They broke and crumbled like a patch of fog as the sword swished through them. Slack-jawed, he watched them fade and vanish.

From the doorway, Sharajsha smiled.

Thongor released his breath explosively.

"So it was you!"

"I thought you needed some help," the Wizard said.

Thongor wiped the clammy sweat from his face.

"Aye, that I did—but did you have to scare the guts out of me in doing it?"

"They were not real—mere phantoms of the mind. Come, yon fat-bellied priest will raise the alarm. We must be gone, and quickly."

"And the Sword?"

Sharajsha raised it from beneath his cloak. With

his rune-enchanted hammer he had beaten the glowing-hot stone into a long rough blade. Along its jagged, uneven edge blue sparks crawled. The hard star-steel shimmered with power, and the air about it quivered.

"It must be impregnated with the virtue of lightning next, and that we can only do upon Sharimba, the Mountain of Thunder, a thousand *vorn* from here. Let us leave!"

They went down the curving stone corridor, Thongor leading. He padded like a jungle beast, every keen sense alert for danger. Surely, the alarm would have spread by now! But no sound, no call, no tread of running feet could he detect.

And they came to the secret door. Even as Sharajsha reached for the concealed catch that opened the panel, the vengeance of Yamath struck. The Wizard gasped, clutched at his throat and fell, sprawling on the cold stone.

Thongor, too, staggered. He braced himself erect, holding on to the wall with one hand while he struggled against the mysterious influence that theatened to overwhelm him. It was as if a sudden and irresistible sleep was coming over him.

Sharajsha struggled to speak. "Vapour . . . drugged . . . do . . . not . . . breathe. . . ."

Then the Wizard was unconscious. Thongor held on to the edge of sleep with iron strength, fighting against the dark tides that rose to engulf him, with every atom of strength his powerful body held. With swimming eyes he sought for the hidden catch, numb hand pawing the blank stone in vain. His lungs ached for air. His mighty heart laboured within his panting, straining chest. Then, just as he had reached the farthest limits of his strength, his finger touched the hidden catch and the door swung open—striking him off balance.

He fell full-length on the floor, the impact driving the air from his lungs. Instinctively, he took a breath. The narcotic vapour entered his lungs, and Thongor lost consciousness, there in the sacred crypts of Yamath under the great Fire Temple of Patanga.

On the Altars of the Fire-God

"The naked virgins on thine altars plead
As scarlet flame on pallid flesh doth feed!
Lord of · the Fire, drink down, young lives like
wine—
Hearts, limbs and breasts—their very souls—are
thine!"

The Rituals of Yamath

SUMIA HAD known fear, but never before had she known despair. Was it days—or weeks—since they had come to drag her off to these dungeons in which she had been chained ever since? She did not know. When the Yellow Druid, Vaspas Ptol, had first pressed upon her his suit of marriage, she had coldly and proudly refused. That had been at the death of her father, Orvath Chond, Sark of Patanga. And for months afterwards, the oily Prince of the Druids of Yamath had continued to offer her marriage . . . and each time his humility lessened and his arrogance increased, in direct proportion to the rise of his power over the city.

At last he believed his position secure and had come into her bed-chamber unannounced, to force himself upon her. The young Queen had resisted him and drawn a knife and threatened to slay him if he so much as laid one cold hand upon her. Vaspas Ptol had withdrawn, snarling threats, and that very hour his soldiers had seized her and brought her to the secret dungeons below the Fire Temple. Here had she languished since that time. At first she had feared that Vaspas Ptol would force himself upon her, bound and helpless as she was. But he had not come near. Nor had the guards offered her any discourtesy, only silence to her pleas and indifference to her commands.

She knew now that the Yellow Druid was waiting for the Festival of the Year's End, when living sacrifice would be offered up to the dread Lord of the Fires. That sacrifice, Sumia knew, would be herself.

And the festival would be this very night.

It was now about dawn. She had been unable to sleep all the night, and now in the first hours of morning, just as she was drifting off to sleep, the shuffle of footsteps and the clank of accoutrements awakened her. Guards were coming down the hall.

The lock clanged and the iron door of her cell opened. Into the cell two men were dragged. They were both unconscious, hanging limply from the hands of their captors. Sumia watched in puzzlement as the guards chained them to the opposite wall. Neither of them were Patangans. The taller and younger man wore the common leather clout and trappings of a mercenary soldier-of-fortune, and the old, bearded man wore the long robes of a sage.

"Who are these men you bring to my cell?" the Princess demanded. The captain of the guards smiled thinly.

"Two fellow-sacrifices, destined for the Altar of Fire beside yourself, O Princess!"

"They are not Patangans . . . what have they done?"

The Otar shrugged, "They were found in the sacred cavern of the Eternal Fire, which their presence desecrated. When they were discovered, the young one fought, slaying six guards and insulting a Druid. Vaspas Ptol has condemned them to the Altars. He believes they were in the crypts attempting to steal the offerings and treasures, but were interrupted before they could get to them."

The guards locked Thongor and Sharajsha to the opposite wall of the cell and left, leaving Sumia to her silent vigil beside the two unconscious men.

Thongor awoke from the sleep-vapour first and stared around. The first thing he saw was a slim young girl sitting on a wooden bench across the cell, looking at him. She appeared to be about eighteen, with hair of glossy blackness, which poured in thick waves of curls down her slim back. Her skin was of almost marble whiteness, tinged with creamy colour. Had she not moved, Thongor would have thought her a statue, for her features and limbs were so flawless they seemed to have been chiselled from pure marble. Her face was a slender oval under the glossy mass of curling black hair. Beneath thin, curving black brows her eyes were dark wells of light.

Beneath his gaze her cheeks darkened from soft cream to the same rich colour as her soft lips.

"Where are we?" Thongor asked.

"In the dungeons of Vaspas Ptol, Arch-Druid of Yamath, God of Fire," the girl answered.

Thongor tested his chains. His wrists were riveted to the wall against which his back was pressed. The old Wizard, still unconscious from the narcotic vapour, was similarly bound beside him. The girl wore a copper ring about her slim waist, fastened to a ring set in the wall with a slender copper chain.

Thongor told her his name.

"I am Sumia of Patanga," she said

He regarded her with surprise.

"The daughter of Orvath Chond, Sark of Patanga? Why is the Sarkaja of Patanga chained to the wall of the dungeons of Patanga?"

"Because I scorned to wed Vaspas Ptol," the girl said proudly. "He approached me when the Sark, my father, died some seven months ago. I have refused him, not just once but many times. But his power has grown in Patanga, until at last he feels strong enough to dispose of the Sarkal office and rule the city himself."

Thongor nodded, sourly. The greed and lust for power of the Druids was familiar enough to him. If ever he managed to get out of this place and complete his task with Sharajsha, perhaps he could set about uprooting some of these depraved priesthoods.

"Tonight is the Festival of the Year's End," Sumia said. "We shall be sacrificed to Yamath tonight, while Vaspas Ptol watches."

"That may be as it will," Thongor growled. "The old man captured with me is a powerful magician. Doubtless he will have something to say about that—as will I, if I ever get my hands free and close them about the hilt of a sword. But tell me, will the people of Patanga really stand by and watch their rightful Sarkaja die on the altars of Yamath?"

"Yes. They are helpless before the might of the Druids. Vaspas Ptol has this city in the palm of his hands. They fear his magic, and his cruelty . . . and he has played so cunningly upon their superstitions, that he rules them through their dread of Yamath, the false God he worships."

"Is there no one, then? No relative—no lover?"

She coloured again, lifting her head proudly. "I am the last member of the House of Chond. Nor have I any lover. I am here in this dark place because I scorn to marry any man whom my heart has not chosen!"

She fell silent then, nor could Thongor engage her in any further conversation, for she answered only briefly. Shrugging, he made himself as comfortable as possible against the wall and went to sleep. His recent exertions and lack of rest took their toll. He slept soundly for some hours, facing death with the healthy contempt he always displayed towards danger.

When he awoke again. Sharajsha had also come to his senses. The old man had either breathed in a more powerful dose of the sleeping-vapour, or else his advanced years made him more susceptible to its influence, for he had out-slept Thongor for hours. Now he was conversing in low tones with the girl.

Thongor yawned and stretched, and greeted his comrade.

"Use some of your magic, Wizard. Get us out of these chains and put a sword in my hands."

Sharajsha sighed.

"They have fastened my hands apart," he said. "I cannot touch my sigils to use them. We shall have to wait until the guards free my hands."

"When will that be?"

"The noon hour, perhaps, when they come to feed us."

"They will not feed us," Sumia interrupted. "Since we are the destined sacrifices of Yamath, we shall fast until the Hour of the New Year, so that we may be pure for the burning." Thongor cursed.

"It is bad enough to sacrifice us to their filthy god—must they starve us as well?"

The girl stared at him, and laughed. "Never before have I heard a man complain more about his empty belly than about his approaching death!" she said.

Thongor shrugged. "That I am a prisoner condemned to death I cannot help. And I refuse to worry about that which I cannot change. But I still feel hungry!"

"Cease to think of your belly, and think about escaping from this place," Sharajsha said.

"Perhaps Karm Karvus will try to rescue us," Thongor said. The Wizard thought about that for a time, then shook his head doubtfully.

"How can he know where we are kept? He is in the same position that I was, when you were captured in the Scarlet Tower of Slidith. And he will doubtless do what I did in his place, simply wait above the city for a sign."

The day passed very slowly. But gradually it did pass. And after many hours the shadows of evening began to gather and the hour of the Festival approached. Guards came to bring them to the great Fire Temple. Thongor had planned to fight once his chains were off, no matter what the odds, but he had no opportunity. Before he was loosened from the wall, his wrists were manacled together, as were his ankles. And Sharajsha's arms were similarly bound behind his back, where he could not employ his magic rings.

The Wizard met Thongor's questioning gaze with a little shake of the head. Thongor released a deep breath.

"Well, then, at least we shall die in the company of friends," the Northlander said lightly.

"Come!" the Otar of the guards said, mockingly. "The flaming Altars of Yamath await you, his most honoured guests. And the God is—impatient."

They went out of the cell, ringed about with swords, up an endless flight of stone stairs and down corridors of polished yellow stone . . . into the great Hall of the God.

It was a gigantic circular room. Above their heads, the enormous dome lifted for two hundred feet, its curved vastness broken by huge windows of coloured glass. At the far end of the circular hall, Yamath stood. It was a brazen idol ten times the height of a man. The bald head was horned and a great fanged mouth grinned beneath eyes in which small flames had been lit. The Altars were held in the cupped hands, which rested on the idol's lap. They were also of brass, hollow, and beneath them furnaces raged. They would be chained nude upon these Altars and roasted alive. Thongor set his jaw grimly as the guards marched them across the vast floor towards the towering idol.

They passed between rows of Druids in yellow robes, chanting praises to their obscene deity. Magnificently-gowned nobles watched silently, behind the rows of Druids. Thongor saw pity on the faces of many of them, as they watched their young queen go towards death. But the nobles were unarmed, and each priest wore a long, curved sword. And archers were ranged along the walls.

Sumia walked proudly, head high. Her small, slippered feet carried her without faltering to the base of the idol. There the Yellow Arch-Druid halted them. Vaspas Ptol was gorgeous in jewelled robes of yellow velvet, but the beauty of his apparel could not hide the vulture-like greed of his cold eyes, his hooked beak of a nose, nor the cruel twist of his lipless mouth.

"Here you make your choice, fair Sumia," the Yellow Druid rasped coldly. "Accept either my embrace and reign beside me on the throne of Patanga ... or go into the fiery embrace of Yamath, from whence there is no return. Choose well!"

Sumia, from her small height, smiled up into his leering face and laughed lightly.

"I would rather die a thousand cruel deaths than marry a man I do not love," she said. "And for you, Vaspas Ptol, I feel no love. Only contempt—disgust—revulsion. You are not a man, you are a cold fire that scorches and slays everything that lives about you."

The Druid's cold eyes went ugly. He gestured to the priests and they bore her forward. Thongor and Sharajsha were brought along beside the Queen.

The idol of Yamath was fashioned so that it seemed to be sitting upon its crossed legs, tailor-fashion. The Altars were contained in its lap, and the draperies of brass that clothed it in the likeness of a loin-clout were formed into a flight of steps that led up to the Altars. It was up these steps that the three prisoners were led. There they were turned about, facing out over the crowded hall and bound upright to metal poles that passed through their manacles. Here they would stand in full view of the celebrants, while the Altars were heated.

Drums boomed and trumpets rang out, echoing through the domed hall. The Arch-Druid ascended a platform beside the idol's gigantic knee and began to sing-song the rituals of preparation. Having chained the three sacrifices to the poles, the guards lifted a trapdoor that led into the interior of the idol and went within, to stoke the furnaces that would heat the brazen Altars red-hot.

Thongor said nothing to his comrades as they gazed out over the audience. But the great muscles in his back and arms began to swell. The slim pole passed up his back through one link of his wrist-chains. He was pulling upon that link with his terrific strength, seeking to snap it.

Bowls of incense were set afire, sending swirling, pungent clouds of purple smoke through the room. Gongs and drums thundered. Lines of yellow-robed figures dipped and swayed in a barbaric dance.

"I cannot reach my sigils," the Wizard said softly. "If my wrists were not bound apart I could touch my magic rings and free us in an instant."

"We are bound too far apart for me to reach your hands, or perhaps I could remove one of your magic rings and you could tell me what to do," Sumia said.

Thongor grunted. "Courage!" The great muscles of his broad shoulders were leaping and writhing like bronze serpents as he applied the terrific leverage of his arms against the unyielding iron pole.

He had built the strength of those shoulders with long years of exercise . . . swinging and heaving through a dozen wars, hefting the mighty broadsword of his homeland. Now he needed every atom of iron strength those muscles contained!

Behind them, the altars were heating up. Thongor could feel the heat against the skin of his bare back. His muscles knotted and tensed with supreme effort. Droplets of sweat stood out upon his brow and slid wetly down his powerful arms.

Now three priests were coming up the steps to

fasten them to the blazing Altars, now red-hot behind them. As they gathered about Sumia, preparing to strip her naked—there was a sharp gasp from Sharaj-sha.

"Thongor—look! Upon the platform where the Arch-Druid stands! Your sword and the Sword of Nemedis as well. .. . . They must plan to hurl our possessions into the flames of Yamath along with us!"

The sight of his familiar, beloved Valkarthan long-sword lent extra strength to Thongor's efforts. His face grew congested and purpled with the intensity of his straining muscles.

One priest took hold of the collar of Sumia's gown. He ripped it away. One pearly-white breast was laid bare. Sumia stared ahead of her, her dark eyes enormous in her pale face. A shiver of anticipation ran over the faces of the priests. The Druid licked his thin lips and reached out—

A sharp metallic *twanggg* rang out, so loud that it was heard the length of the hall. The strained and weakened link had at last yielded to Thongor's barbarian thews!

His hands free, Thongor was upon the priests with one cat-like bound. He tore the Druid's hands from Sumia, picked the kicking and squirming figure up with one hand to throat and one to crotch, and— *hurled him upon the Altar*! There was the sizzling, crackling sound of human flesh frying and the shrill unearthly screech of the Druid filled the hall with terror.

Thongor hurled the other two priests from the platform, dashing them against the stone pavement far below. Then he was loosening the chains that bound Sumia's slim wrists. Using the iron hilt of a priest's dagger for a lever, he snapped the links of her manacles and freed her—then turned to do the same for Sharajsha.

Pandemonium raged. The temple became a madhouse of whirling, shouting people. Priests and guards rushed up the steps of the idol. On the platform near the god's knee, Vaspas Ptol called down the curses of Yamath upon the blasphemers who had dared fight free from the embrace of the Fire God.

Thongor put the dagger into Sumia's hands and shoved her towards Sharajsha, so that she might free the old Wizard while he turned to fight off the oncoming priests. He sprang to the head of the stair and kicked the first priest in the face, smashing his nose into a bloody ruin. The Druid fell back, knocking others from the stair.

Thongor snatched up his fallen sword and hewed down two guards. His savage war-song thundered through the shrieking chaos of the hall as the red sword rose and fell. He slew four before the blade broke upon a steel helmet. He flung the broken hilt at a man's face and sprang back from the rush. Now his fists swung out, cracking heads and spilling bodies off the platform. Boiling with a berserk fury, he swept men off his back and hurled them upon the fiery Altars. He seized one guard by the ankles and swung him around like a great living club of flesh, knocking a dozen men flat. He released the man and he whirled across the room, thudding into a knot of priests. The barbarian was in his element—a good fight.

But Sumia had freed Sharajsha, and the Wizard joined the battle. Bolts of white fire sprang from his lifted hands, setting yellow robes and guards' cloaks afire. Sharajsha took the head of the stair while Thongor retreated, and cast bolt after bolt of magic flame down, clearing away the guards.

Thongor poised at the edge of the idol's knee—and dived into space. He landed cat-like upon the platform where Vaspas Ptol crouched, white with fear and outrage. From the platform Thongor took up the half-completed Sword of Nemedis and his own great blade. Before he could turn to slay the priest, the Yellow Druid had picked up his skirts and jumped off, landing in the milling crowd below. Thongor roared with laughter.

Then the great windows of coloured glass far up in the dome above crashed in with a deafening music of splintering glass and a thick rain of knife-sharp shards fell into the crowd. The gleaming silvery shape of the *Nemedis* floated over the hall, her weird form striking mad panic into the hearts of the people, priest, guard and noble alike. The air boat descended to the idol's knees, where Sharajsha, his grey beard flying and lightning spewing from his upraised hands, had held the stair while Thongor went to recover the enchanted sword.

As the hall rapidly emptied of its terror-stricken

throng, who fully believed the very Gods had descended in transcendent wrath, Sharajsha helped Sumia aboard the floater and then they descended to floor level so that the giant barbarian could clamber aboard.

Thongor sprang on to the deck, magnificent in the fiery light, naked and grinning, smeared with blood, brandishing a sword in either hand.

"Karm Karvus!" he roared. "Never was I so glad to see your face! Make greeting to the Princess Sumia, rightful Sarkaja of Patanga—and, for the love of the Gods, let us get out of this place, before Sharajsha brings the roof down with his magic lightnings!"

He tossed the magic Sword at Sharajsha and they clung to the rail as Karm Karvus set the *Nemedis'* prow up-rising sharply into the air. Within a few seconds they were out through the shattered windows and over the crowded, panic-filled streets of Patanga.

"North and west, Karm Karvus," Sharajsha commanded. "We must reach the Mountain of Thunder before dawn, for the old year has ended and the new year begins—and in just days the Dragon Kings will summon the Lords of Chaos from their dark abode beyond the Universe, to trample all of Lemuria down into the slime from which it rose!"

The glittering craft rose steeply in the air and shot over the roofs and towers of Patanga, vanishing into the northern skies, bearing with her the hope of the world.

The Mountain of Thunder

"He beat them back with a broken blade,
    half-drowned in the roaring tide,
But the great black spear drank deep
    as it sank in Thungarth's naked side.
Yet ere the Son of Jaidor fell, and ere
    his strength should wane,
The Broken Sword of Nemedis had clove
    the Dragon's brain."

Diombar's Song of The Last Battle

SUMIA SANK exhausted on the cabin's small bunk, pale and trembling from the danger and exertion. Sharajsha brought her a cup of wine and they rested as the floater drove through the midnight skies and Patanga gradually diminished behind them.

"Wizard!" said Thongor, "I'll taste a goblet of that drink as well, and so, no doubt, will Karm Karvus." The Tsargolian locked the controls and turned to join them.

"I feared I had looked my last upon the both of you," he said, relieved. "When you did not signal for me to descend and pick you up I became fearful for your safety. And as the hours passed, I became certain you were captured—or slain. And then I saw the excitement of the great Fire-Temple and even at my height some noise of battle came to me. So, on the chance that it might be Thongor of Valkarth behind this commotion, I descended and entered the Temple."

"Well for us that you did, Karm Karvus," the Valkarthan grinned, tossing aside his empty goblet. "And now, bid greetings to our guest, the Royal Sumia, rightful Sarkaja of the City of Fire. Her throne has been usurped by a Druid, even as was that of the late but not lamented Drugunda Thal!"

Karm Karvus bade the Princess welcome, and turned to Sharajsha.

"Were you successful in forging the Sword before your capture?" he asked. The Wizard nodded.

"Aye, or else why journey to Sharimba, the Mountain of Thunder?" He displayed the jagged blade proudly. The Princess, who had recovered from her exhaustion, and who now looked lovelier than ever with the warm rose colouring her creamy pallor, had been attempting to follow this conversation.

"Was it that you stole this sword?" she asked. "Was that why you were condemned to the Altars beside me?"

Sharajsha explained to her the plot of the Dragon Kings and related something of their adventures until the present, as Thongor cleansed and bound his wounds.

As they ate an impromptu meal from the floater's stores of dried meat and cheese, Sharajsha questioned her.

"Since it would be foolish in the extreme for you to return to Patanga, Princess, where shall you go? Has the House of Chond friends in nearby cities?"

"Nay," she said wearily. "Let me accompany you on your voyage. The yellow Druids have extinguished the houses that might have welcomed the daughter of Orvath Chond."

"It will be less dangerous for you to return to the arms of Yamath God of Fire, than to venture with us, Princess," Thongor said. "We voyage into unknown perils, for we know not what forces the last of the Dragon Kings can bring against us. In the long ages they have spent in their remote and hidden fastnesses, Gorm alone knows what terrors they have brewed."

"I should rather remain with good and true friends," she said firmly. And 'that was that. No arguments they could muster forth could sway her stubborn determination.

All were long since wearied, and with this matter resolved, they made ready for slumber. The only bunk was given to the Princess of Patanga, and the others stretched out on the cabin's floor, rolled in their cloaks. They slept for hours, as the floater hurtled ever northwards. Below her silvery keel the curving, silver ribbon of the River Saan traced a winding path through forest and field, past the walls of Kathool and on, ever farther and farther north, into the foothills of the Mountains of Mommur.

Thongor awoke after a time and took the controls, lifting the slim craft above the towering piles of rough black rock. These mighty ranges of mountain and cliff were at the very heart of Lemuria. They stretched from the marshes of Pasht in the West to the plains of the Blue Nomads in the East, a stupendous wall of rock almost two thousand *vorn* in length. And winding through their labyrinthine way, the great Saan curved for league after league, to reach at last the dark waters of the Inner Sea of Neol-Shendis, wherein the Dragon Isles were known to lie.

Some hours after dawn the cloud-wreathed peak of Sharimba loomed before them. It was the mightiest mountain of all Lemuria, towering above its brothers like a black giant standing amid squat dwarfs. Thongor roused his companions and they broke their fast, as the floater measured off the *vorn* between them and the Mountain of Thunder.

Sharajsha bade Thongor guide the air boat to a landing somewhere near the crest of the black mountain.

"Only I, armed with the powers of magic, may ascend the uttermost peak of the mountain," he explained. "For when I call down the lightnings of heaven to embue the Sword with power, those not protected by great craft and magic skill would be charred to ash . . . such are the powers I must invoke."

The black wall of rock loomed sheer before them. Then the Princess cried: "Look!" Thongor followed her pointing hand and saw a gap in the rock and suddenly a flat table of stone appeared, where some unimaginable convulsion of the earth's crust had shattered off a portion of the peak. There he brought the *Nemedis* to rest. Sharajsha clambered out, his long, wide-sleeved robe of grey and his long grey mane of hair fluttering in the howling winds that swept the mountain. In one hand he grasped the Sword. In the other was a small pouch of scarlet *photh*-skin containing magical instruments. Standing there, the naked sword in his hand, the wild landscape of cloven black rock and wind-torn sky behind him, he suddenly became a weird and mysterious figure, removed from the common range of mankind.

"Await me here," he commanded. "From this point I must ascend to the peak unaccompanied, so do not come after me for any reason."

"What will happen now?" Karm Karvus asked.

"Once I have reached the topmost pinnacle of the mountain, and have evoked the powers of the Throne of Thunders, the sky will darken. Clouds will gather, blackening the very sun. Then forth from the clouds, bolts of lightning will assail the peak, filling the sky with flame. But the Sword will drink the lightning even as the green things of the earth drink the sunlight, and with every bolt the power of the Sword will grow, until at last it has been charged to the final degree with energy. Fashioned from stone—forged in fire—drenched in the powers of the air, it shall command the elements of nature."

"And—water?" Karm Karvus hazarded.

"For water it shall drink deep of the accursed blood of the Dragon Kings," the Wizard said, and he turned and slowly began his ascent of Sharimba.

Standing in a row together, they watched his thin, bent figure until it dwindled above them and vanished among the jagged rocks of the mountain-peak.

Thongor spat. "Sorcery! Give me a good blade and a strong arm. That's all the sorcery one needs to fight an enemy!"

Sumia shivered, staring up at the cloud-wrapped peak.

"What will happen—when we face the Dragon Kings with the enchanted Sword?" she wondered aloud. Karm Karvus shrugged.

"I know not, Princess. Perhaps the Sword will disgorge the lightnings upon which Sharajsha will feed it. However, we shall soon see. For within mere hours, now, the destined time will come when the monsters will seek to summon their Dark Lords from the unknown realms that lie beyond the stars— beyond the very Universe itself!"

Silent, Thongor watched Karm Karvus talking to the girl. The slim, courtly noble and the lovely Princess could converse as equals—but he was a rude barbarian! Broodingly he observed her slender loveliness . . . the great, curling fleece of black hair, slim, pale limbs displayed in creamy glimpses through the rents of her tattered gown. Never in all his years had he seen such loveliness in a woman. Lemuria had not seen her like since the fabulous days of Queen Zandarla the Fair. He turned away and, setting his back to them, he stared out over the fantastic gulf of broken stone and wind-torn vapour, illuminated by the level, ruddy shafts of the morning sun.

Ah, well! Such beauty was not for the likes of him, a rough warrior more used to trading jests with Death at the tip of a dancing blade, than exchanging courteous phrases with high-born ladies.

Sumia screamed!

Thongor whirled, his longsword flashing into his hand, his fierce golden eyes searching the rocks for an enemy. The shrill screams of the Princess were echoed by a metallic screech whose reverberations raised the hairs on Thongor's nape—*a grakk!*

Down from the airy gulfs winged the terrible lizard-hawk, a very twin of the one that had attacked him days ago over the jungles of Chush. Its wriggling, scaled snake-body was mailed in fantastic yellow and brown. Its furred and bat-like wings darkened the air. At the end of a long serpentine neck the hideous head reached for the girl. She was running towards the floater, slim legs flying. The head swooped towards her—grim, hooked beak clashing hungrily, cruel scarlet eyes blazing with insatiable hunger beneath the indigo-blue crest of wild, bristling spines.

Shouting, Karm Karvus whipped out his Tsargolian rapier and raced to aid the Princess. Roaring his deep-thoated war-cry, Thongor exploded into action. One lithe bound brought him to the side of Karm Karvus and together they plunged their steel into the writhing body that hung in mid-air upon thunder-beating wings, while the long neck quested after the fleeing girl. But even sharp steel could not penetrate the tough leathery hide, and their blades slid harmlessly off the horny scales.

Sumia cried out again as the loose rocks twisted under her feet—and then she tumbled down, helpless beneath the darting beak.

Thongor sprang astride her, roaring. Clenching the sword double-handed he swung the mighty blade with the full power of his iron thews. His edge met the clashing beak and batted it to one side with the impact. The lizard-hawk screeched deafeningly. He swung again, his blade shearing off the crest of blue bristles. Karm Karvus came up to join him.

"Get the Princess into the floater!" Thongor commanded.

"And leave you——!"

"Do as I say, man—quick now!"

As Thongor battled with the monster flying reptile he was aware of the girl being taken from beneath his legs and glimpsed Karm Karvus bearing her in his arms to the safety of the *Nemedis*. But he was too busy to do anything but fight—and fight he did!

The grakk was gigantic—fully as large as the air boat. Its beaked head was almost as huge as Thongor's entire body and the tremendous muscles of its sinuous length could have torn him to ribbons in an instant, could it have seized him. But the giant Valkarthan danced over the mountainside, leaping away from each plunge of the hissing head, battering at it with great blows of his blade, never still for an instant. He roared and shouted at the hovering thing, holding its attention lest it should leave him and pursue the Princess and Karm Karvus.

Its great membraned wings beat the air like the booming sails of a ship, the wind buffeting Thongor. With great hewing strokes he tried to sever the armoured neck, to extinguish one of the scarlet eyes that blazed into his, mad with fury. But the steely scales resisted his blows as might the granite mountain itself. Thongor knew it was only a matter of time until his feet would strike a loose rock, bringing him down sprawling . . . or before he should fail to dodge the swinging head and be caught in the vice-like grip of that slavering yellow beak. He fought tirelessly.

And then one clawed foot seized him, dragging him down. Hooked claws the size of curved scimitars bit into his leather trappings. Dragged by the hovering monster, his skull hit a boulder and blackness enveloped him.

In the cabin of the floater, the Princess stifled a cry when Thongor fell. Breathlessly she watched as the lizard-hawk hovered on thundering wings above the helpless man. Beside her, Karm Karvus gave an oath.

"Stay here, Princess!"

The Tsargolian sprang from the floater's deck to do what he could to save—or to revenge—his friend. But before he could reach Thongor's side, the cruel barbed claw closed about the barbarian's waist and the winged monster rose slowly into the air with the unconscious man dangling from its powerful grasp.

Helpless, Karm Karvus stood beneath, watching as the monster lizard-hawk rose—knowing that at any moment he could expect to watch his mighty friend dashed in the gulf below—or devoured by the ferocious grakk. As the lizard-hawk hovered, it bent its long neck and seemed to sniff at the dangling body.

From the safety of the floater, Sumia clasped her hands to her beating heart. Breathlessly she watched as the bold warrior who had saved her from death faced death himself.

And then the two watched as the lizard-hawk, seemingly satisfied that its prey was either helpless or dead, rose steeply on booming wings. It circled above them, and then slid away over the great gulf.

Still bearing the unconscious Thongor, the grakk vanished towards the east and was lost to their view among the thick vapours.

Karm Karvus slowly slid his rapier back into its scabbard. Bending, he picked up the fallen longsword that Thongor had carried through a hundred battles. With the sword in his hands he returned to the floater.

"Can we pursue the grakk in the air boat?" Sumia asked.

"To what avail, Princess? How could we battle the lizard-hawk, even if we could find it again? And if we could somehow battle it, would it not drop Thongor in order to fight us?"

Sumia bowed her head silently, recognising the wisdom in Karm Karvus' words.

"Nay, there is nothing that we can do, Princess," the Tsargolian said, sadly. "Were Sharajsha here, perhaps his magic could save our friend—but he is far above, where we dare not venture. I doubt not that Thongor has been slain—crushed in the grakk's great claws, by now. Let us be brave and reconcile ourselves to the fact of his death."

And then Karm Karvus fell silent, placing the great Valkarthan longsword upon the bunk. Even in the arena, facing the grinning jaws of death, he had never known a more terrible moment than this— forced to stand by helplessly and watch a friend carried off to a lonely death in the wind-torn skies of Lemuria.

Far above them the skies darkened and the drums of thunder rolled, as Sharajsha prepared the Sword. But neither of them was listening, each one deep in thought.

The Dragon Kings

"As one by one his brothers fell, he raised
    the great Sword high.
He sang the runes to the Lords of Light
    —and thunder broke the sky—
Red lightning flashed—drums of thunder
    crashed—a rain of fire fell
To sweep the Kings of the Dragons down
    to the smoking pits of hell!"

Diombar's Song of The Last Battle

IT WAS the rush of cold wind over his naked body
that roused Thongor to consciousness. When his eyes
opened at last he was staring straight down into a
sheer gorge of black stone that lay two thousand feet
beneath him. His long black mane flowed on the cold
wind, obscuring his vision. For a moment he thought
he was dead, and that the War-Maids were bearing
his spirit to the Hall of Heroes beyond the world.

But then he realised he was still alive. The warm
blood leaked from his brow, where the boulder had
struck his head, and his waist ached abominably, as if
he was being crushed in a giant vice. Craning his
neck about, he discovered his terrible predicament—
and for a moment, even Thongor of Valkarth felt his

heart falter beneath the icy hand of Fear.

The huge claw of the grakk held him about the middle, as its powerful wings bore him far above the Mountains of Mommur. His sword was gone—he was completely unarmed. Were the lizard-hawk to simply open its claws, he would hurl down helplessly two thousand feet to smash his life out in a bloody smear against the black rocks far below. Never in his long, adventure-filled life had the Valkarthan felt so alone—so completely helpless.

Yet he had the comforting knowledge that the princess was safe, and that the battle against the Dragon Kings would still go on, even though he was not there to stand beside Sharajsha when he faced the Lords of Chaos.

Since there was absolutely nothing he could do to lessen his predicament, Thongor simply composed himself and lay still in the grakk's clutches. Rather than exhaust his strength in hopeless fighting, he resolved to await the turn of events and do nothing until some avenue of escape presented itself.

The grakk might have been flying for hours for all he knew. It was difficult to estimate the sun's height from his position, but it seemed near the zenith. After a long time, the grakk suddenly slowed in its flight, and hovered above the range of mountains. Then, sliding through the misty air in long slow spirals, it began to descend.

Out of the murk a slim needle of rock emerged. The lizard-hawk swung down towards it in sweeping circles, hovered for a moment, great wings checking its flight—and dropped Thongor.

He fell helplessly, the landscape whirling madly about him for a terrifying moment or two, then landed with stunning impact upon a thick bed of something that crackled beneath his weight. Dazed, he lay still, not daring to move lest he dislodge himself. There seemed to be no broken bones. Overhead, the black shape wheeled to the left and began to spiral up, soon becoming lost to sight.

Thongor was lying in a shallow depression filled with dry branches and stiff leaves that rustled as he sat up. All about was sky—torn mist, driven by the whistling wind—the distant peaks ringing him in. He crawled to the edge of the matted branches and peered over. Below, a sheer wall of rock fell sickeningly straight down as far as the eye could see.

He turned to see if it was the same on the other side—and looked into a flaming red eye. Three snake-tailed little monsters, only slightly less than his own six and a half feet, were glaring at him a dozen feet away. Their hideous bodies were covered with small red and yellow scales and from the base of the long snake-like necks, peculiar stumps protruded. They had curved beaks and four cruelly-clawed limbs.

In a flash, Thongor realised his terrible position. He had been dropped by the giant grakk, only to plunge into an even worse nightmare. *He was in the grakk's nest!* This tangled mat of dry branches and leaves was the nest of the mother grakk; and those three scaly horrors glaring at him were the offspring of that monstrous parent, who had borne him home to feed the babies!

They had not attacked him yet, probably because they were unused to food that still lived. But now one of the little monsters waddled across the nest towards him, beak clashing, hissing like a jet of escaping steam. Thongor clapped one hand to his side—the longsword was gone, dropped on the slopes of Sharimba, when the grakk had seized him. He stared around swiftly, darting glances here and there about the nest, searching for a weapon. Almost at his feet lay a long white bone, scarred with beak-marks, one end broken off in a jagged, saw-toothed edge. He snatched it up and sprang to meet the infant monster.

Its beak snapped at him hungrily, but Thongor knocked the head aside with the flat of his arm and drove the sharp bone into the long snaky throat. The scaly armour of the grakk-cub was not as tough as that of the full-grown lizard-hawk, but it was tough enough, and the pointed bone merely ripped a long shallow gash in the creature's neck. It welled with thick, evil-smelling fluid.

Then its claws were upon him, its full weight bearing him down as the long neck snaked with distended beak to tear out his throat. Thongor protected his head and throat with crossed arms—doubled up his legs and kicked violently—hurling the thing out of the nest. It went scrabbling over the edge—squalled piercingly—and vanished far below.

But now he faced two more hissing horrors. He

drove his bone-sword straight into the open jaws of one and ducked while the other's beak snapped-to above his head, catching a few strands of his hair. Balled fists lashed out, smashing the chest of the first one. It raked his chest and belly with sharp claws, drawing thin scarlet furrows down the bronzed flesh. Then it gurgled and fell away, tail thrashing violently. The pointed bone had gone through the back of the throat and had penetrated what little brain the grakk possessed, paralysing it.

But Thongor had no time to observe the death-throes of the second, for the third was upon him with flashing claws, bearing him over backwards beneath its squirming weight.

Thongor fought his way to his feet, forcing the squalling grakklet back with smashing blows. Then his mighty hands locked upon its pulsing throat, just below the clacking beak. Muscles swelled and writhed in his broad shoulders like giant snakes. The grakk struggled violently, twisting its long neck, but slowly, remorselessly, his hands closed like iron bands, crushing the monster's thoat. Its scrabbling forelimbs raked him from nipple to hip, razory talons slashing red lines through his flesh. Thongor gritted his teeth and bore the slashing pain.

Gradually, the grakk's struggles lessened in their intensity. Its scarlet eyes glazed. A bobbling froth of slimy beast-blood oozed from its straining, gasping beak. With every atom of strength in his terrific back and shoulders, Thongor crushed the life out of the thing and cast its quivering corpse from him.

He stood, panting, recovering his breath, ignoring the blood that flowed down his chest and belly. Then he prowled the nest from side to side, seeking an exit. On all sides, nothing met his probing gaze but sheer, cliff-walls of black rock, wet from the hovering veils of mist.

He was marooned atop a steep pinnacle of smooth stone. *Unless*—

On one side of the nest the wall was broken. A narrow ledge jutted from the needle of rock . . . but it was thirty feet below the place where he stood. Thongor examined the rock wall between himself and the ledge. It was as smooth as glass. To attempt to climb down it was pure madness—to try jumping to the ledge was completely impossible, for it jutted from the wall only a foot wide. If he missed, he would be smashed to jelly thousands of feet below. And yet—to remain here was to die. Within hours—perhaps within mere minutes—the grakk-mother would return to the nest.

The floater soared through the skies above the Mountains of Mommur. Within its small cabin, Sharajsha, Karm Karvus and the Princess Sumia sat, tensely watching the landscape flash past beneath them.

It was less than an hour since the Wizard had come down from the Mountain of Thunder, bearing the great Sword. Now the weapon lay across Sharajsha's knees, its ice-blue blade quivering with unleashed power. The electric tension of a storm cloud seemed to hum within its mysterious metal blade, and a faint halo of sparks appeared and vanished about the point. The Sword was ready.

Sharajsha had been shocked and saddened to hear of Thongor's terrible fate. But there was no time to waste on a fruitless, hopeless search for the giant barbarian. Only hours remained before the Moment of Conjuration. Already the afternoon sun was declining towards the west. And of what use to search out their dead friend? His broken body lay in the bottom of some rocky gorge . . . or his clean picked bones. They must speed to their desperate rendezvous with time!

Far below them the endless leagues reeled past. Thanks to the Wizard's improvement on the original design, the great coiled springs drove ceaselessly. No time need be wasted while slowly toiling to rewind the coils. The spinning blades of the rotors bit into the thin, cold air of the heights, thrusting the *Nemedis* ahead, her needle-sharp prow slashing through emptiness, pointed ever east into the gradually dimming sky.

Now the great mountains fell away and the silver ribbon of the Saan, Lemuria's greatest river, came into view, threading her winding way through the sheer black gorges. Ahead on the very horizon, like a dull iron shield, the glistening expanse of the Inner Sea could be glimpsed. Locked in by miles of mountains, walled with sheer cliffs of smooth, solid stone, the sea of Neol-Shendis had not been seen by a human eye in ages. What secrets—what dangers—

hid within her mist-shrouded shores?

The three adventurers ate, rested, waited out the time. Sumia sat upon the bunk, her pale face lifted to the forward window. Before her eyes drifted pictures . . . visions from her memory. She remembered the bold, laughing face of Thongor. She saw again his fighting grin and heard his thundered war cry as he had held the entire ranks of Patanga at bay, there on the brazen knees of the God of Fire. She saw again his mighty longsword whirling in a glittering arc, cutting into the snarling faces of the Druids, a crimson spray of blood-droplets flying from its blurred path. She remembered the deep chest, the powerfully-moulded arms and shoulders, and the long, quick legs of the Valkarthan adventurer. It was hard to believe that such animal vitality, such inexhaustible strength—was extinguished.

"Thongor. . . ." As she whispered his name, she felt again that strange, unfamiliar stirring within her blood.

Now the wet grey beaches of the Inner Sea of Neol-Shendis were beneath them. Waves of cold dark water washed against the lone sands. No sea-birds called along these empty strands of shore, which had never felt the foot of man. No small, scuttling creatures of the sea's edge marked the sallow, greasy foam that the sliding waves left behind as they retreated, gathering strength to assault the land again.

The westward skies were reddening between the black notches of the mountain walls as they approached the Dragon Isles. There were four of

them, bleak, wet clumps of jagged black rock looming above the swilling waves. Clinging to the crest of
the largest isle was a fantastic castle of black stone,
towering into the thick mist like a giant from the
dawn ages.

The rotors died and the air boat sank silently,
gliding like a ghost through the vapour, coming to
rest upon a spur of glistening rock. The three clambered out, anchoring the floater securely to a sharp
angle of rock. They made their way along the narrow
crest of the spur and on to the main island. Hidden
by the fog, they melted into the shadows below the
walls of the black castle and vanished from sight.

Sumia clung to the wet rocks, stunned by the
flying spray and the hollow booming thunder of the
surf. Karm Karvus set a strong hand beneath her
slim arm and helped her up.

"We must be silent now," Sharajsha cautioned, his
grey robes making him almost invisible in the thick
fog. They followed him along the black wall. Above
them, looming to a stupendous height, the frowning
wall towered. The castle was built of enormous cubes
of rough-hewn black stone, each block taller than a
man. This cyclopean work of masonry looked oddly
wrong—as if its dizzy angles and queer curves had
been designed according to some geometry of another
world—the weird architecture of nightmare, curiously disquieting to the eyes. A dozen yards below
the ledge upon which they walked, the surf pounded,
icy spray splashing about them, chilling them to the
bone.

They came to a great gateway, open and unbarred, facing the eternal waves. It was unguarded—empty. Sharajsha unsheathed the magic Sword and gestured them forward. He went on first into the black maw of the portal, the naked Sword glowing in his hand.

And then—madness!

The fog suddenly writhed—boiled—congealed, and monstrous black forms loomed out of the mist towards them. Karm Karvus' rapier sang as he whipped it from its scabbard. Sharajsha lifted the blazing blue length of the Sword—but out of the whirling fog a fantastic black figure appeared, eyes like sparks of living green flame burned coldly within its mis-shapen head. A glittering black hand clamped upon Sharajsha's wrist with crushing force.

The Sword fell in a dazzling arc from his nerveless grasp. Sparkling with blue flame it whirled out—down—and into the thundering waves. It vanished in the boiling chaos of black water and white foam.

Sharajsha, helpless in the iron grip, gave a thin, despairing cry. He raised the other hand, magic rings sparkling into life—but an uncanny force struck him and he sank unconscious.

Karm Karvus sprang, sword bared, straight at the weird black phantom figures, still veiled behind the swirling fog. From the lifted black hand of one a sizzling spark of white energy darted, seizing his sword. He stiffened at the thrilling electric shock, and crumpled unconscious on the wet stone floor.

An enormous black hand closed upon Sumia's slim

shoulder. It had seven fingers, each tipped with a black talon, and its cold hard flesh was covered with an intricate pattern of tiny glittering scales.

From the black shadow that had struck Sharajsha down, a cold hissing voice spoke with a weird mockery of laughter ringing in its sibilant tones:

"What fools, to think that our magic would not warn us of the approach of their flying ship! Their lives shall be spent upon the Great Altar amid the Ring of Monoliths in the hour when the stars come forth—to feed the growing power of the Lords of Chaos, Who will need such life-energy to cross the intercosmic gulfs. Imprison them until the appointed hour—and remove from the old sorcerer his sigils of power. We shall see their white faces again at the Hour of the Opening of Space!"

The cold, hissing voice ceased, and dark lumbering figures stepped forth from the cold mist. But before her eyes could make out the details of those awful forms, Sumia's proud spirit failed, and she sank into merciful unconsciousness.

The Lords of Chaos

"Lords of Chaos dark the sky:
  All the Sons of Men shall die.
Dragon-rune and blood of men:
  Portals ope—to close again?
Naught can make the Portals fade,
  Save the Sword by lightning made."

The Scarlet Edda

THE ONLY way down was—down! Thongor turned from the edge of the grakk-nest and began the unpleasant task of skinning the two infant monsters. With their scaly hide he could fashion a rope, and with its aid, reach the narrow ledge far below.

It was hot, filthy, difficult work. With no sword or dirk, he had to rely upon the strength of his hands and the sharp points of broken bones. He wore out many, but the grakk-nest was littered with many years' accumulation of bones. He regretted the loss of his black cloak, which he could have torn into strips in a fraction of the time it took him to rip the hide from the hawk-lizards. But there was no use bemoaning what was lost.

He skinned them in long strips, pausing from time to time so as to break off another bone, giving him a sharp point to work with. The fresh hides stank and he soon became beslimed with beast-blood from chest to knee; but he grimly tightened his jaw, ignoring the stench and filth, and laboured on.

When the hides were removed from the carcasses, he knotted the long strips together and fastened one end of the makeshift line around a protruding knob of rock. He tested it for strength, and when he was satisfied the line would hold his weight without slipping or breaking, he swung himself out over the edge and started down the sheer wall of rock. Dangling thousands of feet over the abyss, he resolutely bent his mind on what he was doing and did not allow himself the luxury of being afraid.

The rawhide strips were wet and slippery in his hands. His chest ached where the claws of the hawk-lizards had razored it. Howling winds rising from the gulfs below buffeted him from side to side; but slowly, steadily, he descended the sheer rock-face until his toes touched the ledge. It was only inches wide. He looked to both sides—the ledge ran both ways, and he had no way of telling which direction would lead him to the easiest descent. So he simply chose blindly and started inching along the ledge to the left, still clinging to the line.

Just as he reached the point where he had to relinquish the line, the ledge widened. He let go of the knotted length of hides and, clinging with both hands outstretched to the face of the cliff, he inched his way along blindly. After a few terrible feet, the ledge widened a bit and angled downwards steeply.

Foot by foot, yard by yard, Thongor descended. Here his barbarian heritage served him well. Where a city-bred man would have faltered—would have lost his balance and perhaps fallen—Thongor continued his descent with nerves of steel. A boyhood spent clambering over the glass-slick glaciers of his icy Northland home had given him a good head for heights and a gift of feeling out minute toe-holds with infinite patience.

Just the same, it took him an hour to descend two hundred feet. But from there he could move swiftly and surely, standing erect.

The mists were too thick for sunlight to penetrate, but from the position of the sun the last time he had seen it, he estimated the time was late afternoon. And that meant he had been travelling for hours. He was completely lost. An hour before, as he had been clambering along the skyline of the ridge of mountains, he had glimpsed the black, cloud-wrapped peak of Sharimba when the rushing winds had parted the mist-curtain. It had stood on the very horizon, many hundreds of *vorn* from where he stood. The tireless wings of the mother grakk had indeed carried him far from his friends.

Sharimba was west of him, which placed the Dragon Isles somewhere east. He had turned east and continued along the skyline. Surely, by now, the Sword would be finished, and his friends would have gone on to their rendezvous with the Dragon Kings, thinking him slain.

All afternoon he had moved swiftly over the plateau, and as the light began to wane he found an easy descent and came down into the valley of the Saan. Now Thongor was racing with a long-legged, tireless stride along the rocky brink of the river. Thrice he had paused at the limit of his strength to bathe in the swift cold water, and drink his fill, and rest a few precious moments before continuing on towards the east. All he knew was the Saan eventually emptied into the Inner Sea of Neol-Shendis, and so he followed it.

He was loping along a crumbling slope of broken stone when an ear-splitting hiss froze him into a crouch. Rising from the foaming waters was a sleek, saurian head with fanged jaws agape. Red eyes gleamed evilly into his.

Thongor's hand closed futilely on his naked hip, where only an empty scabbard hung. Ah—what he would have given for a sword! But there was not even a stick to defend himself with, and the rocks were either too huge to lift, or too small to harm the unknown monster of the river. It rose out of the seething water, droplets running down its long snake-neck. Fore-claws crunched and squeaked on the wet stone shelf that was the river's brink, as it dragged its length up on the land.

Thongor ran.

Perhaps the thing could not run fast enough to follow him—but, no, it had great hind-legs like a gigantic hound. He did not know what the green-scaled and yellow-crested reptile was . . . some nameless monster of the mountain rivers . . . but it was hungry.

It followed him for about a *vorn*, gradually nearing. Its size made it too big for the rocky shelf and so it moved slower and more carefully than he. He ran. And just as he reached the black mouth of an unexpected cave, it caught up with him.

The blunt, arrow-shaped head came hissing down to him and the thick forepaws clawed towards his flesh. Thongor set his back against the smooth rock, bracing himself with his arms, and kicked out with all the strength of his legs. His feet caught the river-reptile squarely in the chest . . . and because its heavy weight made it slip and scrabble insecurely in the loose rock, he bowled it over. Hissing with fury, it fell into the river with a great splash of water. Thongor whirled and darted into the cave. Within seconds he was lost in pitch-blackness, but he stumbled on. He did not know what other creature might challenge him for possession of this cave, but it could not be worse than the thing from the river.

The cavern dove steeply downwards and Thongor followed it. For a time he could hear the river-monster behind him, blundering into the stalagmites and squalling with rage and frustration, but eventually only silence came from behind him. Doubtless it was waiting for him to return—so he simply went on forwards into the darkness.

After some hours the cavern floor slanted upwards again and he began a long, slow ascent. It must be night by now, he thought grimly. The Night of Destiny. Every step might very well be carrying him farther and farther from his companions. But there was nothing to do but go on.

He came out of the cave so suddenly, that he clung to the edge dizzily, staring down where cold black water exploded in a fine mist of white spray against fanged black rocks. *The Sea*—!

And when he emerged fully from the cavern to look about him, he found an even greater surprise. He was not on the shore, but on a steep black rock in the *centre* of the Inner Sea! All around him stretched dull water under a dark, cloud-covered sky. He could see the dim black bulk of the shore-line behind him, stretching off until it faded into the darkness.

The cavern had run under the floor of the Sea, rising to the surface of this tiny islet. Letting the cold wet air bathe his exhausted body, Thongor stood atop the small mound of stone and gazed around. These were the Dragon Isles, beyond a doubt, for there to his left only a few dozen yards across the water rose a larger isle, its black heights crowned with a fantastic castle of rude ebony stone. The Luck of the Gods had directed his steps.

He descended to the edge of the water and clung there for a moment before plunging in to swim to the other island. Blinding sheets of spray drenched him, and then the cold shock of icy water on his tired flesh was equalled by another shock—he stared down into the foaming madness of the exploding water.

A sword.

The dim light caught the glittering length of its blade. It was under several inches of water, wedged sideways in the grip of the rocks. His hand itched for the familiar shape of a sword-hilt. He dived in and came up with the sword in his hands, and clambered back upon his rocky spire again, squatting in the narrow cave mouth while he examined his find. The light was very dim—it was hours into the night, perhaps near midnight—but even by the faint light he could not fail to recognise that strange, jagged blade, glittering with power.

The Sword of Nemedis!

"Gorm!" Thongor swore. He knew by this token that his friends had either been captured—or slain—for only force could have made Sharajsha relinquish the magic blade for whose creation they had spent so much time, and faced so many dangers. His face went bleak, his eyes cold. If Sharajsha was taken, what of Karm Karvus? What of . . . Sumia!

He stared up at the grim black castle whose weird turrets and battlements loomed far above him into the mist, rising from the nearby island that lay only a short swim across the cold, swirling water.

Within that dark fortress his friends lay, either helpless captives or murdered corpses. Cold fire flared within his strange golden eyes and his teeth flashed in a grin that had no humour in it. He slid the Sword into his empty scabbard and dived from the rock into the black, icy water.

If he were too late to rescue them, he would at least be there to avenge them. The Sword would reach its destined place upon the fated hour, whether man, monster, or even the Dark Lords of Chaos stood to bar his way!

For hours Sharajsha, Karm Karvus and the Princess lay in the chill, dank darkness of a bare stone cell. Few words passed between them, for there was nothing to say. Sharajsha was stripped of his magic implements and sigils, nor did any of them possess a weapon, save for the small knife Sumia wore concealed beneath a strap of her trappings. The slow, weary hours marched past as the grim stars rose gradually to their long-awaited positions. Many times, Sumia's thoughts returned to Thongor, whom she believed slain. She could not define the strange emotion that rose within her breast when she thought of the brave Valkarthan warrior who had saved her from a terrible death.

Karm Karvus and the Wizard talked together quietly for a time.

"What will they do with us?"

"Even as the chief of the Dragon Kings said, as you have reported his words to me. They will lay us upon the black stone altars of their three grim gods and there we shall die . . . our life-energies going to feed and strengthen the Lords of Chaos."

"A savage death, fit for such fiends," Karm Karvus said. "Ah, if I had a sword! Or if Thongor were here. Together we would fight, back to back, and show the Dragon Kings how men should die, standing upright and facing death, not bound to a stone table."

"Aye," Sharajsha agreed, soberly. "Or had I one sigil left—one talisman! But Sssaaa, the Lord of the Dragon Kings, stripped me bare."

"Sssaaa? Was that the thing that seized you and made you drop the Sword?"

"Sssaaa is the Lord, or Arch-Priest, of the Dragon Kings. He is the one who led them here when the Black Citadel fell to the Sons of Nemedis, thousands of years ago. . . ."

As the fateful stars slowly returned to their appointed spheres, the time came. The three bade farewell to each other, quietly, with dignity. Then the great door clanged open. Sumia gasped. It was the first time they had seen the Dragon Kings close and clearly. They stood, half again the height of a man, erect upon great bent hound-like legs. From massive shoulders sprang short arms, clawed and powerful. The neck was longer than that of a man, and the head was blunt-muzzled, expressionless. Slit eyes of cold green flame blazed beneath a brow whose misshapen and un-serpentlike bulge denoted a human, or perhaps more than human, intelligence. The Dragon Kings were scaled and black, torchlight glinting with minute points of light along the glassy armour of their hideous bodies. They had long, heavily-muscled tails.

But somehow the chill gleam of malignant, intelligent fire that burned in their eyes made them more terrible and fearful than the beasts their bodies suggested. A beast slays from instinct, from the natural urge of hunger . . . but these creatures could be as cruel as a man.

And it was frightful to see beasts wearing man-like trappings. For the glittering black-scaled bodies were accoutred in thick belts and harnesses like men, with pouches and jewelled ornaments and weapons of monstrous and uncouth design. Sumia's proud spirit quailed, yet she held her head high and did not deign to let the things read fear either in her expression or in her bearing. The blood of a hundred kings flowed in that small, graceful body, and never was good breeding displayed better than in that dark hour, by the last of the House of Chond.

"The Hour is nigh; come forth, manlings," the cold, sibilant voice of Sssaaa commanded. Karm Karvus glanced at Sharajsha and read his tired nod, and so did not resist. Those massive arms and shoulders held strength before which even the giant thews of Thongor himself would seem puny.

They strode out of the cell and into a vast hall. The light that they had glimpsed from within the cell did not come from torches, but from strange spheres of thick glass which hung by thin chains from the domed ceiling, shedding a sharp, unwavering red light. They had no time to examine the weird achievement of the Dragon's science, for they were marched forth by their grim captors, down the giant hall and through a mighty rotunda where doubtless the Lords of the serpent-folk held council.

Here, too, the strange red lights burned without flickering, and a great circular table of some unknown green-grey metal stood, with strange-shaped chairs spaced about it. The black stone walls were hung with peculiar tapestries of woven metal-thread, depicting scenes alien to a human eye. Strange gardens of fleshly-shapen flowers and weird, fronded trees, under which the Dragon Kings of a bygone age disported in peculiar garments too complex to be noted merely in passing. A thrilling glimpse into a world lost millennia ago, when the black Dragons were the masters of the Earth, before the coming of man.

They went out of that room and into a vast, circular courtyard under the stars. The wall of the black fortress ringed them about, and in the centre of the courtyard rose a vast ring of black pillars, nine in number. And beyond that, an outer ring of twenty-seven more. They were nineteen feet tall, carefully hewn of the same black stone—huge brooding menhirs, looming up into the thick mists that hid the skies. They stood like the legs of gaunt black giants whose upper bodies were hidden behind the clouds. Now and again a rent appeared in that heavy veil of evilly-coiling mists and a faint star burned ominously through. The great monoliths were carven with Dragon runes—odd, twisting arabesques worked in bold relief. Of the three humans, only the old Wizard could read their terrible message, and he shuddered and dropped his eyes.

A score of Dragon Kings stood within the court, each bearing a light-sphere within its black claw, and a strange helm of red metal upon its misshapen brows. They had formed a wide column and as the three humans were led down their ranks they burst into a hissing chant in their ancient tongue. The ceremony was beginning.

They were led into the centre of the double ring and there a great circular slab of ebony stone lay like a vast table. Manacles of red metal were fastened to their wrists and ankles as they were forced to recline.

"Courage!" Sharajsha said.

The archaic, hissing chant roared around them, rising and falling like the waves of the sea. Above their heads the floating wreathes of mist twisted like vaporous tentacles about the uncouth pillars. Stars winked through the tattered veils.

Now drums rumbled to the patter of clawed hands, sounding in an alien counterpoint to the sibilant chant, their muted thunder echoing Sumia's pulse beat with a slowly-rising tempo. She shut her eyes.

Sssaaa strode forward into their vision. He ascended the altar-disc and walked to the centre. The three humans were bound at equal distances from one another, their heads together near the centre of the stone. Sssaaa took his place there, towering above them. He lifted his great glittering arms to the sky.

"Iao-Thamungazoth!"

The chanting rose towards full cadence, its surf-roar booming. The serpent drums sounded in long rolls, rising and falling. The mist coiled between the standing stones that seemed to hover giddily above them, no longer upright. Sumia felt as if the very dimensions of space were being bent awry before the flowing rhythm of the unearthly chant.

Sssaaa thundered another name, its other-earthly syllables echoing from the reeling monoliths. The chant rose behind him in sibilant music.

Suddenly the fog seemed to stream towards an area of the sky directly above the altar-stone. Long wisps and ghost-like wraiths of fog sped between the black fingers of the columns to meet in the centre, coalescing into a thick ball of darkness. Sumia shuddered at the clammy caress of the fog-fingers as they streamed over her body. She felt a strange vertigo, as if the Earth were spinning beneath her. The circular wall that ringed the courtyard seemed to be revolving about her like a vast black wheel.

Sssaaa called upon the third dreadful name, and with a sudden flash the skies were clear. Above them the stars burned in strange patterns—*slowly—one by one—turning red*. The centre of darkness had by now absorbed all of the fog, but it still seemed to draw upon the surrounding air with a terrible, insatiable suction. A breeze quickened about them, chill winds plucking at their garments and lifting Sumia's long raven tresses. The wind blew directly into the ball of darkness . . . as if the atmosphere of the Earth were being drawn through some unknown orifice, into the endless hungry vacuum of unknown space.

The drums rose into a wild, maddened cacophony and the clangour of metal bells sounded on all sides, where the Dragon Kings had formed into a loose circle, dipping and weaving and swaying upon their great splayed hind-paws. Dizziness poured over

Sumia as the Earth seemed to sway in rhythm to the Dragon dance.

Above, the red stars of the destined Hour blazed.

The wind arose to an icy gale, howling like a mad thing among the swaying monoliths. The circle of blackness grew, as if feeding upon the air and mist.

Now the carved hieroglyphs upon the menhirs glowed with a mysterious red luminance . . . and the curious helms of the Dragon Kings and the chains and manacles upon their helpless victims also glowed with the unknown radiation. Sumia felt a chill, icy tingling spreading through her body.

The sensation of vertigo rose and fell, even as the rhythm of the hissing chant, the drums, and the waxing and waning of the crimson star-fires.

Suddenly all was silent.

Silence, complete and dead, as though they had been instantly stricken deaf. The Dragon Kings froze. The wind, the swaying vertigo—ceased! The very Universe seemed to hang suspended—to hold its breath, as if awaiting some terrible signal, some final act—

Sssaaa drew slowly from his harness a great black sword with a pronged blade. The Sword of Sacrifice. He bent over the Princess and she stared upwards, uncomprehending, frozen. The forked point descended towards her breast . . . and suddenly she knew that within seconds it would rip through her soft flesh and scoop out her living heart, hurling it aloft into the hovering Heart of Darkness above. She felt an icy paralysis clamp down upon every nerve, every muscle. She could not scream, although her mouth fell open. She could not tear away her terror-frozen eyes from the horrible sight as the blade descended to touch her motionless breast.

And behind them, Thongor laughed.

It was a rich, deep, full-thoated laugh, warm and human. Its warmth seemed to crack the ice that bound them all; Sssaaa jerked uncontrollably, lifting his massive head to stare with wild green eyes. Sumia turned her head and saw Thongor across the courtyard, standing with spread legs atop the black wall. A cold hissing began among the Dragon Kings, and Sssaaa straightened.

From behind him, Thongor lifted the Sword into view.

Sssaaa screamed like a jet of escaping steam. The great circle of monsters broke and milled, in a tangled confusion.

The Sword blazed with light, not the clotted scarlet of the Dragon's magic spheres or the glowing symbols on the black columns, but a clean blue fire that seemed to burn through the murk and blur about them, dazzling and cleansing as the light of high noon.

He pointed the Sword at the centre of the altar-disc, where the Lord of the Dragon Kings stood, the Sword of Sacrifice raised high.

Thunder cracked!

A jagged, sizzling blast of lightning arched from the Sword to the black blade of death. The black sword melted, searing the Dragon's cold black claws.

He flung it from him, shrieking with maniacal fury.

The second bolt caught Sssaaa upon his weird helm of blood-red metal. It heated to the melting-point instantly, and the great black body arched with the unbearable shock, tearing its muscles loose from its bones with the terrific impact of the thunderbolt. His brains fried, body blasted, the Lord of the Dragons fell twitching spasmodically to the black pavement.

The Dragon Kings broke, screeching. Some fled with wild loping strides for the citadel; others raced to pluck the giant barbarian from the walls. But the Sword was alive with fire now, like a stupendous blue-white torch. Bolts of crackling fire sprang from it, playing over their scattered ranks in a dazzling shower of electric fire.

A stream of thunderbolts landed among the columns, shattering some and toppling others. The black forest of stone fell, crushing many of the Dragon Kings beneath the weight of the monster monoliths.

Bolt after bolt poured into the motionless globe of darkness. The air quivered, exploding with thunder. The whirling chaos of the courtyard was lit with flashes of blinding white fire. The heavens cracked across, and cold rain and howling wind came drenching forth . . . as if, in the evil paralysis of Dragon-magic broken, outraged Nature was striking back in all her raw, elemental fury. Blinding, stinging sheets of cold rain flooded down in a wild deluge, and the roaring song of the wind arose into a shrieking madness about them. Through its rage, came the deep, ringing voice of Thongor, chanting the mighty, barbaric music of Diombar's ancient song:

" . . . .and thunder broke the sky—
Red lightning flashed—drums of thunder crashed—
  a rain of fire fell
To sweep the Kings of the Dragons down to the
  smoking pits of hell!"

Before the terrific storm of blue-white lightning, the swirling centre of darkness broke—shattered—crumbled into fragments that rapidly dispersed and were gone. The storm rose. The noise was deafening. Wind and rain; the thunder of falling columns, and above them all, the iron-throated song ringing out in brave verses of victory

"He beat them back with a broken blade knee-deep
  in the roaring tide,
But the great black spear drank deep as it sank
  in Thungarth's naked side.
Yet ere the Son of Jaidor fell, and ere his strength
  should wane,
The broken Sword of Nemedis had clove
  the Dragon's brain."

The rain was falling so heavily that through its glassy curtains the blundering, stumbling forms of the Dragon Kings were but dark shadows against the blinding flashes of exploding lightning. The dazzling bolts caught at wall and turret, clung twisting for a few instants, then vanished as a rain of broken rubble slid down into the court. Now lightning blazed in the skies above them lighting the entire heavens in terrific sheets of flame, almost as if Father Gorm, the Lord of Lightning Himself, were partaking in this last, epic battle against the Dragon Hordes. And sky-bolt and Sword-bolt flamed together, striking down the Dragon Kings one by one.

Before this whirling chaos Sumia swooned for a moment, or an hour, for when she next opened her eyes the storm was vanishing with the same swiftness as it had begun. Under the clean light of the stars the destined cycle passed, the black citadel lay in wet smoking ruins, the ringed monoliths either fallen or raising only broken stubs to the clear, calm sky; now the full moon was emerging softly to wash the Earth and sea with her pure, serene light.

From his lonely post on the ruined wall, Thongor stood as if exhausted, the no-longer-glowing Sword held in his hand. Through the calm stillness of the night, he sang softly the last verse of the ancient song:

"Thunder rolled in the crimson sky; the War-Maids rode the storm
To bear the soul of Thungarth home to the halls of Father Gorm.
The Age of the Dragons ended then, where the seas with scarlet ran.
Though the cost was high, the prize was great And the Age of Men began..."

Then Thongor came down from the crumbling

wall, and across the rubble-choked courtyard to the broken disc of the altar. And the keen blade of the enchanted Sword bit through the links of their chains and they were free, and Sumia felt at last the strong, gentle arms of Thongor the barbarian around her, bearing her up carefully, holding her against his naked chest, her head against his heart.

"You are not dead," she said, and Thongor shook his head, wild black mane falling across his bronzed shoulders.

"Nay, Sumia, I live," he said quietly. And his golden eyes looked down into her eyes, which glimmered like dark stars. She made no further answer, for a great weakness rose within her, but her perfect lips curved a very little in a faint smile ... and then she sank exhausted into the darkness of a deep and healing sleep, cradled in the Valkarthan's powerful arms.

And the Age of Men began....

Epilogue

THE *Nemedis* floated a few feet above the ground before the cavernous entrance to the subterranean castle of Sharajsha the Great. Standing beside the ladder, Karm Karvus of Tsargol, Princess Sumia of Patanga and Thongor of Valkarth were making their last farewells to the old Wizard, before flying on to the adventures that yet awaited them in the days to come.

"Since you will take no pay or reward for the time you spent in my service, Thongor, accept then this slight gift from a friend," Sharajsha said, pressing into Thongor's hand a small package. The Valkarthan examined it curiously.

"It's a mere trinket, an armlet of gold, a token of our adventures together. Yet keep it by you, for someday it may come in handy."

Thongor nodded and thrust it within the pocket-pouch of his trappings.

"The time has come for us to say farewell," Thongor said. For two weeks, since their return from the Dragon Isles, the three adventurers had been the guests of the Wizard of Lemuria in his underground palace. There they had slept, rested, and feasted. Sharajsha had shown them his marvels, and they had talked through the long evenings discussing their adventures and the perils through which they had safely passed. Again and again Thongor recounted how the waves had lodged the Sword of Nemedis below the mouth of the cavern where he emerged to find it beneath his eyes, and Sharajsha solemnly declared it was the work of the Gods . . . perhaps of Father Gorm, Himself, for nothing but an act of the Gods could have brought the sleeping powers of the Sword back to life there in Thongor's hand as he stood upon the wall of the black citadel. For Thongor knew not the runes and Words of Power with which the Wizard had planned to set into action the enchanted blade.

"The Gods smiled upon our quest, and I feel within my old bones, Thongor, that they shall watch over you and that yours is a charmed life." Thongor smiled with the healthy scepticism of the barbarian, but made no comment.

But the Valkarthan was not made for leisure, and after some days he chafed to be away finding adventures again. The others found him again and again fondling the hilt of his beloved longsword, which Karm Karvus had preserved for him when he had lost it. So at length the hour of farewells came around.

"Take the floater, for it is yours," the Wizard said. "And I shall keep the Sword here, for vast powers are still slumbering within it and in the hands of the unwary, or the greedy, should it fall into such hands, it could work terrible things out in the lands of men. Here I will keep it safe, for I see within the misty future a time when once again the powers of the Sword will be needed. When that far-off hour comes—whether to you, or to your children, or to your distant descendants a thousand years from this hour—when the Sword is again needed to lift against the Forces of Darkness, you shall take it from my hand."

They nodded, not truly understanding, and Thongor stirred restlessly anxious to be gone.

"Fare you well, Prince of Karvus. Where will you go?" Sharajsha asked.

The Tsargolian bowed. "For me, who have no home, I shall follow the trail of Thongor, for I know that wherever he is, there will be fighting aplenty!"

They laughed, and Sharajsha turned next to salute the Princess of Patanga.

"Farewell to you, my Lady Queen," he said. "And what road shall you take?"

She smiled and shrugged lightly. "For that I have no home either, I too shall follow Thongor. For where my brave warrior is, there is my home as well." And her smiling gaze met the warm golden eyes of the barbarian.

Sharajsha turned then to the Valkarthan.

"And fare you well, Thongor. Where do you plan to journey?"

The Valkarthan grinned the reckless, fighting grin that they had seen before when he laughed in the teeth of danger. He slid his longsword from its sheath and kissed the blade, saluting Sumia.

"I? Why, Wizard, I shall return to Patanga,

where a filth-hearted Druid soils the throne of my Princess—and that throne I shall win back for her—aye, and a place beside her for myself!—unless my right arm and my Northlander steel have both lost their strength."

And with that they entered the *Nemedis*, Thongor lifting Sumia over the low rail and bounding to the deck with one stride. The Wizard withdrew to the mouth of his cavern as the air boat floated up into the morning sunlight, circled once, and sped out over the dense jungles of Chush, bound for Patanga, the City of Fire.

Fantasy Fiction in Tandem editions

By John Jakes

A warrior's sword against the sorcery of ancient evil

Brak the Barbarian	25p
Brak the Barbarian—The Sorceress	25p
Brak the Barbarian—The Mark of the Demons	25p

By Andre Norton

'Rich, brilliant, superbly imaginative and fully adult pure fantasy' *Lin Carter*

Witch World	25p
Web of the Witch World	25p
Three Against the Witch World	25p
Warlock of the Witch World	25p
Sorceress of the Witch World	25p
Year of the Unicorn	25p

By Ursula LeGuin

Hugo and Nebula Award winning writer

Planet of Exile	25p
Rocannon's World	25p

By John Norman

The Chronicles of Counter-Earth ..

Outlaw of Gor	25p
Priest-Kings of Gor	30p
Nomads of Gor	40p
Assassin of Gor	40p
Tarnsman of Gor	30p

Science Fiction in Tandem editions

Planet of No Return Poul Anderson 25p
Man must search for colonies beyond the stars, but can
he find a permanent home there?

Let the Spacemen Beware Poul Anderson 25p
. . . 'what makes the inhabitants of a strange planet
tick. . . . Trust Poul Anderson to get a new twist into
the story.' *Morning Star*

Vornan-19 Robert Silverberg 30p
Charlatan, agent of chaos – or witness that their world
was not doomed? Could anyone in 1999 ignore him?

The Time-Hoppers Robert Silverberg 25p
Every human need was fulfilled in the 25th century, yet
they still yearned to escape

Hawksbill Station Robert Silverberg 25p
Banished from the complicated world of the far future
to the barren emptiness of the remote past

The Man in the Maze Robert Silverberg 25p
Solitary and embittered, hiding from the loathing of his
fellows, he must be lured out of his refuge to save the
world

Light a Last Candle Vincent King 25p
'Vivid stuff, a tale of internecine strife between mutated
and modified people in the far future.' *Edmund Cooper,
Sunday Times*

Farewell, Earth's Bliss D. G. Compton 25p
Their past was Earth, their present a colony on Mars –
and their future?

The Time Mercenaries Philip E. High 25p
They were a thousand years out of date, and the planet's
only chance to defeat the alien invaders

Donovan's Brain Curt Siodmak 25p
Doomed by disease, mangled in a plane crash, there was
no doubt that Donovan was dead. Yet his brain lived!

Hauser's Memory Curt Siodmak 25p
'. . . a fast thriller . . . first-rate science fiction with a
contemporary bite.' *Birmingham Post*

Name ....

Address ....

Titles required ....

....

....

....

....

....

....

....

- -

The publishers hope that you enjoyed this book and invite you to write for the full list of Tandem titles.

If you find any difficulty in obtaining these books from your usual retailer we shall be pleased to supply the titles of your choice—packing and postage 5p—upon receipt of your remittance.

WRITE NOW TO:
        Universal-Tandem Publishing Co. Ltd.,
        14 Gloucester Road,
        London SW7 4RD